NEVER

RIPE

____

John Owen Smith

NEVER RIPE
First published 2002

Typeset and published by John Owen Smith
19 Kay Crescent, Headley Down, Hampshire GU35 8AH
Tel: 01428 712892
E-mail: wordsmith@johnowensmith.co.uk

ISBN 978-1-873855-37-9

Printed by CreateSpace

NEVER RIPE

Short Stories and Rhythmic Writings

John Owen Smith

Contents

1. Serried Rows
2. Gael Force
3. Down the Tubes
4. Spotter Jack
5. Batting Safe
6. Away from the Coast
7. Juno Beach and Beyond
8. Winding Point
9. Crime Doesn't Pay
10. Wild Dogs
11. Deep Wells
12. The Alice Effect
13. The Beautiful Game
14. That's what Friends are for
15. Ghost in the Machine
16. Jobsworth
17. Sweet Fanny Adams
18. The Fifth Mary
19. Marzipal
20. Slim Jim
21. Sylvie
22. Presume Nothing
23. Twelfth Night – Act VI
24. I Survived in Grayshott

Serried Rows

How best should I, whose only weapon's wit,
Confront the challenge of these changing days?
Beneath the thin veneer of culture's skin
Lie deep unyielding roots and custom'd ways.

I'll use what sense I have to understand,
Within the province of my nature's skills,
Such base dynamics bred into the bone
As manifest themselves in stubborn wills.

Though never ripe, my fruit must now be picked;
My thoughts, transferred through keyboard into prose,
Must advertise themselves for your delight
Like plums on mongers' stalls in serried rows.

And who can tell what treasures you might find
Inside such fruit, to fill the eager mind?

Gael Force

"Why shouldn't I?"

"No reason. I just don't think you should, that's all."

Night driving, and the small twigs pattering on the roof of the car like hailstones, except that the sky was clear and the temperature mild. We'd excused ourselves early, escaped as Gael put it, from a friend's house-warming party which had seemed set to become an all-night vigil of the hard drinkers, and the country lane leading from the house, sunk by generations of traffic to a depth ten feet or more below the surrounding fields, had sheltered us from the full blast of the wind until we'd joined the main road. I started to accelerate along the deserted dual carriageway.

"Mother wouldn't mind."

"I know she wouldn't mind, but that's not the point."

A strong gust forced us onto the concrete rumble strip for a moment, jerking our minds away from impending argument to immediate reality. Instinctively I swung us back to the tarmac.

"They forecast gales."

"I didn't listen."

Small branches in full leaf littered the road ahead, and I eased into the fast lane to avoid them.

"She'd love it, in fact."

"I said, that's not the point."

A car came towards us along the other carriageway on full beam. "Dip, you sod!"

"Well, what is the point then?"

"The point is that you and I should discuss it on our own first."

"We are on our own."

The dual carriageway was ending, and reflective chevrons ahead warned of the sharp left-hand bend under the railway bridge. I eased off the accelerator.

"I mean, let's not take the idea to her half baked. Let's sleep on it and see if it seems like such a good idea tomorrow."

"Tomorrow never comes."

"Yes it does, it comes in..." I checked the dashboard clock, "twenty minutes time."

She sighed impatiently. "Be serious, can't you." A pause. "Just because it's my idea."

Sodium lamps heralded the start of the town, and the wind seemed to die down a bit. "We'll be home soon, and you can have a good sulk about it. You'll enjoy that."

I ignored the inevitable sharp-knuckled jab to my left shoulder, and we travelled on in silence, through the town and out towards the village, brooding on our own thoughts until we arrived home. I stopped in the road outside and Gael, unbidden, got out to open the gate. The wind was still strong. She held onto her hat with one hand while she fumbled single-handed with the catch, and then let the wind blow the gate open against its stop. I turned in and parked on the drive. She rapped on the window before I'd even got my seat belt off.

"I'll let you shut the gate. Give me the keys to get in."

I locked the car and handed the keys over. She swept away towards the front door, leaning into the gale, while I wrestled with the gate, cursing myself for the hundredth time for not fixing the broken latch. I did the best job I could in the dark, then headed by instinct across the lawn towards the front door. A harvest of acorns had fallen from the oak tree, and with each footstep I scrunched a number of them into the soft ground. "Planting for the future," I thought.

The door was shut, of course, and I had to ring the bell to get in the house.

"Who is it?" she shouted from the kitchen in a pastiche American accent. Obviously not sulking too deeply, I thought.

I looked through the letter box. "Mickey Mouse," I shouted back in reply.

"Not today, thank you Mickey."

"Well, who would you like it to be?"

"Someone incredibly rich and handsome." She came down the hall and opened the door. "Oh well, I suppose you'll have to do. You'd better come in."

"At least I'm available."

"So's yesterday's newspaper."

I gave her a peck and went upstairs to wash my hands after the gate-grappling exercise. Ours was a typical modern three bedroom detached house; that is it had a double bedroom, single bedroom, joke-size bedroom and bathroom upstairs, and a hallway, L-shaped lounge and kitchen downstairs. I took off my jacket and tie (it had been a 'formal' party), threw them on the double bed, kicked off my shoes and came downstairs again.

She'd put some music on—*The Four Seasons, Spring*, I think—and was standing by the sideboard in the dining area of the lounge. The lights were dimmed; could romance be in the air?

"Drink?" she asked as I came in.

I looked at my watch; it was still today—just. "Thanks."

She poured us each a whisky with a little water, and brought them to the sofa in front of the flame-effect fire. We touched glasses, took a sip, and sat down in our familiar places. Outside you could hear the wind gusting, if you listened hard enough through the Vivaldi.

I looked at her, and saw she was gazing levelly at me across the top of her glass. "So?" she said, and left the question hanging with the expression on her face, a frown still on her forehead and lips still rounded.

Obviously she wasn't going to let the matter rest. I tried to remember what had brought it up. The party, as I said, had been a fairly formal affair and we'd been looking for some kindred spirits to talk to, but they seemed few and far between. We'd ended up being cornered by a wine-soaked young Estate Agent, not one given to false modesty it seemed. He'd embroidered a long and involved story of a recent successful sale he'd made—a country mansion; right time to buy; silly not to do it now; conditions never better—and so on and on, for the best part of an hour, until we'd made our escape. Some of the monologue had obviously rubbed off on Gael.

"I like it here."

"Jack, we've been here three years now. It's time we moved on."

"Up, you mean."

"Up what?"

"Up market."

"The time will never be better."

She was quoting from the party. "You should know better than to trust the opinion of a sozzled property dealer."

"He's right though, isn't he."

I'd a nasty feeling that he might be—despite the condition of his brain when he told us. In fact I'd been thinking along similar lines myself over the past few months, but hadn't got round to talking it over with Gael. The gate latch, still broken weeks after I'd first noticed it, was just one indication that I'd started to lose interest in the house. I have a theory that, for most people other than unmitigated '*do-it-yourselfers*', any minor job which doesn't get done within six months of moving into a new place probably never will get done. Maybe Gael sensed I was softening as she carried on pushing her case.

"If mother sold her house and moved in with us, we'd be able to afford it easily." I said nothing, but looked vacantly into my glass. "Wouldn't we," she insisted. A statement, not a question.

Gael's mother is, it goes without saying, my mother-in-law; and while she's not quite Les Dawson material I am, nevertheless, fairly happy to see the back of her at the end of each annual visit. The thought of having her as a live-in lodger…

"And think how useful it would be for baby sitting."

"But we haven't got any babies!"

"That's another thing we need to talk about."

I felt the noose tightening. "Look, one thing at a time, OK?"

"I'm off the pill, you know."

"I said one thing at a…" I did a double take worthy of Brian Rix. "You what?"

"I said I'm off the pill."

I felt this was the sort of information a husband ought to be told ahead of—well, ahead of carrying on doing what comes naturally in most marriages. "You might have told me!"

"I thought you might object."

"You're damn right I might object." Then a sudden thought. "Are you…?"

"Not as far as I'm aware."

"Well, that's something."

I took a long swig and emptied my glass. Gael rose and went to refill it without needing to ask if I wanted more. "Would you mind if I was?"

Would I mind? I thought about it silently. She came back with the drinks.

"Well?"

"Yes."

She looked disappointed.

I said, "Yes, because it's a sneaky way of going about it."

"Is that all?"

"Yes, because it's a sneaky way of going about it, and we can't afford it."

"We can."

We could, too. Or at least, as well as we were ever likely to. We'd both been earning good incomes for a number of years, and had managed to save a reasonable amount.

"And if mother…"

"Ah, back to mother."

"Jack…"

"Now listen Gael, you're mother's not bad as mother's go. But here all the time, living with us…"

"It wouldn't be here."

"Well, wherever. Can you imagine the squabbles in the kitchen? I seem to remember you telling me you weren't the perfect daughter."

"She could have her own kitchen."

"What are you thinking of buying, Windsor Castle?"

"Hampton Court, actually"

She tossed her drink back and went for another. My glass was empty again, and I held it out as she went by. I turned to look at her as she stood there in the dim light by the sideboard. Elegant in a close-fitting party dress. That would all change if…

"You're quite sure you're not pregnant?"

"I told you, I don't think so."

More by luck than good judgement, I thought. She brought the drinks back.

"Thanks."

"But we don't want to leave it until I am, do we."

"Until just now I didn't know it was a possibility."

"Sorry."

Silence as we drank again and toyed with our own thoughts. She'd been pouring the drinks generously, and they'd begun to take effect. She curled her legs up under her in the corner of the settee, and gave me one of those looks…

Then, "I love you, Jack."

* * *

Outside, the wind reached storm force, then became a hurricane. Whole trees in full leaf were ripped from their roots and blown across roads, roofs and railway lines amid a mass of tangled power lines. Slates flew through the air, dustbins danced along streets and dogs howled. But in the lounge, in front of the flame effect fire, Jack was oblivious to all this, succumbing as he was to an altogether different Gael force. And if the earth seemed to move for them, there was every good reason why it should do so.

In the morning, the world awoke to a sudden silence, and neighbours who had hardly talked to each other before stood in groups in the middle of traffic-free roads exchanging versions of their night's horror stories which grew with the telling. Whole new vistas appeared of distant horizons where blocks of trees had fallen like wooden dominoes, all pointing north-east. Some ancient landmarks had disappeared for ever, others could be rebuilt.

But for Jack and Gael, in their own way, the passing of the night had also meant that nothing would be quite the same again. And when the telephones were restored later in the day, Jack's first call was to the local estate agent, and Gael's was to her mother.

Shortlisted by 'Writers News', January 1993

Down the Tubes

Mathias Palmer looked to left and right as snake-like cables writhed along the matt black walls, and junction boxes bulged like pigs in a python's stomach. Last night's visit to the *Dog and Bacon*—better not remember while in train without convenience—but, what an evening! Jackie what's-her-name, you know, the one with the eyes and the pleasant surprise, well she certainly knew how to drink without paying—at least with her purse—and the rest of us harboured that happy-hour hope that we might end up winners. But Dougie came by for her, same as he always does, saying we'd only embarrass ourselves if we tried it, so why not go home till we'd grown, like, six inches. Whatever that meant. And to comfort ourselves we all went down the Doner—well those that could make it—to force down a big one, as Jeremy put it, but then he's a Noily. And some of us even got home without calling for Hughie, but man, was this morning unwelcome!

Two bright lights, and the dark tunnel winding; the hammer of the wheels and the whine of the motor.

At the head of his rocking and bucketing silver-flanked charger, Mathias sat dolefully, wedged in the split-sided bitch of a seat that the Company kindly saw fit to provide for the ease of their drivers; his left hand unconsciously pressed on the lever, his right tapping rhythm and blues on his thigh to the beat of the tortuous track at his feet.

A dip and a weave made the wheel flanges squeal, like the girl at the match when McCarthy went through for the second half winner— she stood with her friend on an upended crate, and we kept them well oiled with a few cans of ale, well you never know do you, they might have been goers—so anyway, she and her friend had a view of the match, which was more than the rest of us packed on the terrace had—all we could see was the backs of old jackets with 'Bomber' in studs or a picture of Elvis—so hearing them shouting, these birds on the beer crate, kept all of the rest of us up with the game and the way things were going—all bouncy if Rangers were on the attack, and like tragic if things weren't quite going their way. Not that most of us cared, we were there for the beer and a day with the lads out in Brighton or Swindon, away from the missus and other calamities, making a Saturday worth waking up for; the football was just an excuse to be absent, and most of the fun happened on the way back.

The coach driver, Bill, used to drink up the *Swan* so he treated us fair, there was no aggravation, and plenty of stops for the ones with a skinful, like twice every hour or more often if needed, and me and Frank Parsons would sit at the back to keep watch on the antics of those further forward. Now Frank, he's a one, never misses a chance, if there's anything going he's there like a shot, so when Des from the Deli who's travelling with us gets up and gets out to examine the roadside, before you can blink there's old Frank in his seat—all smug satisfaction, you've guessed the attraction—it's young Mrs. Des who's the talk of the street—she's come out for a ride we are led to believe, though I don't know that Frank was the one she was after— he's chatting her up and he's not doing badly considering how he's been drinking all day and Melinda, that's her, has stayed stony-cold sober and isn't the type to make light conversation; then in swaggers Des fresh from spraying the weeds, and he's not at all happy to see that his place has been nicked in his absence, still less by the fact it's been filled, as he says, by an overgrown schoolkid who couldn't distinguish, excuse my expression, his arse from his elbow in such a condition. It could have got nasty, but Frank's his own saviour; he tried to get up and fell flat on the floor; so Des, stepping over him, got back his seat again, leaving Frank crawling towards the coach door. One day we'll get wise and feel good in the morning.

Two bright lights, and the dark tunnel winding; the hammer of the wheels and the whine of the motor.

Rumbles and rattles in underground passages; Henry says Dick's going bowling in Battersea, making a party up, see if I'm interested, same as they did once before with some talent, but this time it's serious, no girls invited and stakes of a tenner for winner-take-all. Now it's not that I'm stingy or short of the ready, but bowling with Dick isn't quite what I'm into—I'd rather go home to be perfectly truthful, and that's saying something with t'kids watching telly, but maybe if Tom's got his wheels in some order we'll go out to sample a beer in the country—a nice pint of Young's wouldn't go unconsidered—and who knows, we might find some locals to chat to; a couple of railwaymen out on the razzle should rivet them static— somehow I don't think so! We'll probably end up with cans back at his place and watch some old videos from his repository—that's what he calls it, that old cardboard carton he keeps by his sofa—and get paralytic before I go home.

A lurch to the left and a flick to the right, and Mathias's seat rocked in delicate sympathy; so did his delicate head with the pain... He decided tonight would be one for the abstinence.

Not much to ask for, one night staying home—I might even enjoy it—let's look at it this way, I pay all the rent and the bills and the taxes and what do I get from it?—somewhere to sleep and a plateful of dinner—no sort of a bargain when all said and done, and OK it's my own fault I'm not there more often, but one lounge for all of us isn't exotic, in fact it's a million miles short of acceptable. Still, just one night, we might give it a try, and tomorrow you'll love it— convince yourself Matt my boy—take my advice and live healthy for once. But tomorrow's tomorrow...

At home now, the kids would be screaming and fighting, all wanting the naff plastic game in the corn flakes, and Martha, my dear, would be scraping the toast while she yells out for Darren to shift his butt, nicely, and Colin would moan that his jeans are all dirty and why hasn't somebody bothered to wash them, the postman would knock and the kettle would whistle, the bacon would burn and the smoke from the kitchen would set off the fire alarm—God! what a nightmare; well who'd be a mother with four growing children, he'd seen it all once when they altered his shift, and he made the mistake of not staying in bed and came downstairs to eat with them—never again; it was different with women, they seemed to be built for it, almost enjoy it, but he couldn't cope with it, not if you paid him. For seventeen years he'd been married to Martha, and sixteen of those they'd had kids round their ankles, first Sadie, then Darren, then condom-gone Colin, but that hadn't stopped them, they'd still had two others—at least now there's Sadie moved out with her job, it makes one less...

Yes Sadie, his one little girl, and today she's a lady in smart women's clothes doing things in the city, receptionist somewhere; a good girl our Sadie—who knows, any day she could even get married, well p'raps not just yet, give her one or two years first—a nice steady boyfriend, a ring on her finger and cash in the bank to put down on a terraced—she'll do it conventional, none of your love- ins—a proper white wedding up there at St Mary's or he'd let her know it; and he'd be there with her, in tails and a topper to give her away to the guy who deserved her; they'd walk arm in arm through that single south door—the one you see open on special occasions— and then as the organ began the old anthem, they'd walk down...

The aisle became twin lines of steel, and the nave was a platform jam-packed with commuters, all craning towards him in sullen approval; the roar of the organ was rudely replaced by the rumble and clack of the rattling track as the train came from nowhere to slow down to rest in the light and the space of a stationary place, to the tune of a taped 'Mind the gap'.

Mathias sat staring into the deep darkness in front of him, alone in his cabin and quite uninvolved in the frantic jostling of brollied bodies behind. It always took this long at Waterloo. Waterloo. Forget the name, Matt, cross your legs and think of Barnet. Green lights under the Thames, and the two welcome rings of the bell from the guard. Ease down that lever, let her roll—and let's be off the drink for once tonight, son.

Two bright lights, and the dark tunnel winding; the hammer of the wheels and the whine of the motor; the right hand still tapping to the rhythm of the rails as the six silver coaches crawl under the city, and onward and upward through clay and confusion to Highgate, to daylight, to freedom, relief and fresh air.

The end of a story, the end of a saga, the end of the line.

All change. D'you hear me Mathias Palmer, all change!

Spotter Jack

Outside office hours, in what officialdom calls *leisure time*, but in reality is what life's all about, outside the office, Jack Henshaw spotted stars.

No major personality evaded his persistent quest for yet one more key entry to his champion's collection. Star of stage or screen, or hero of the hour, all sorts were grist for Spotter Jack's unswerving observation. Book in hand, he'd lurk in lanes, stand pressed in crowds, sneak skilfully around giant, joyless jobsworths, just to capture that renowned, elusive autograph. But in this all-consuming passion he was not alone.

For in his street lived Giglamps George, fierce rival for the title 'Catcher King' in Moleshill District's own John Moniker Hancock Club. These two competed neck and neck, stride for stride, acknowledged leaders in their chosen field, while other members wearily resigned themselves to vie for third place in the competition.

Not that they were slouches in their skills, these others, not by any means, but Giglamps George and Spotter Jack were streets ahead. Not only did they stop at naught to apprehend their designated prey, but also spent long hours researching every known statistic of potential quarries. Date and place of birth, their pedigree, what food they ate, which party they supported, what they wore—and so on, taken to the ninety-ninth degree. And all these facts, meticulously listed in appendices, were what in essence separated these two sleuths by miles from all the other jealous members of the Club. It was acknowledged, even by the most inequitable types, that these two tireless diggers after detail, George and Jack, eclipsed the most renowned investigative journalists of the day.

But not content with such supreme acclaim, since playing second fiddle holds no satisfaction for the single-minded specialist, each hero still aspired by devious means to overhaul the tally of the other. Each researched the rules to ascertain the best approach, looked out for loopholes, studied hard to find the most emphatic way to overcome the know-how of the other. Sleepless nights and restless days ensued for each as every angle, every strategy was mentally examined, turned and tested by the probing pair. And in the end Jack Henshaw found his own solution.

As with most successful schemes, in retrospect the answer seemed self-evident. From early days he'd always spotted trains, or aeroplanes, or cars, or anything mechanical that moved in any way. He was, in fact, a keenly deep observer, versed in all the minutiae of mechanisation, and the world could end while he inspected a non-standard riveting pattern in a J5 back-fired boiler plate...

The plan was simple: merge his interests old and new; by thus diversifying his collecting habits, he'd no longer merely chase up living beings, he would now include the names and numbers, height, weight, speed and other detailed data culled from copious notes, on railway engines, cargo ships and other metal-hearted pseudo personalities. By this approach he hoped to raise himself to new and giddy levels in the clash with Giglamps George.

And so we see him stationed by the roadsides, at the airports, by the docksides; anywhere in fact where things of substance could be found and classified by either name or number. He wrote their details lovingly within a private, feint-lined, spiral-bound, hard-backed black notebook, nestling by his Thermos, sandwich box and camera in Grandpa Henshaw's khaki gas-mask case. No variant of livery, of lettering or coach configuration passed the eagle eye of Spotter Jack without the fact becoming catalogued and classified for later avid, detailed contemplation in the quiet seclusion of his solitary evenings.

On the road, he knew the country, county, borough, town and date of every passing number plate; the model, make, capacity and cost of every motorised conveyance. Airlines, too; he had their details handy, knowing range and payload, facts and figures of each plane they owned, and reeling off *ad nauseam* stop-over points and scheduled flight times getting you from A to B by way of Timbuktu in time for tea.

And, as it happened, though his plan had not anticipated such an outcome, he discovered by this operation new and varied personalities, the human sort that is, whose autographs he could incorporate along with all the others. Not just station-masters, engine drivers, captains of the fleet, and other such employees at their work, but also those more generally honoured personalities who happened to turn up while he was waiting patiently on Platform 2, say, for some new or specialized configuration to arrive from distant parts. Such opportunities were swiftly seized, and autographs elicited from startled household names who thought their inauspicious entry to the town could not conceivably be noticed. These, Jack estimated, scored as bonus points to be awarded in his favour.

Came the day at last of Moleshill District's AGM. The ritual of chairman's speech and treasurer's notes and votes for officers and all that tedious mandatory business passed, and then the moment of the year arrived as Mr Hepplethwaite (Hon Competitions Secretary) cleared his throat and started to announce the names of this year's winners. Well, you could have heard a feather drop. Third place had been announced, awarded to—it doesn't really matter who—and now the crowded hall was hushed to hear which rival had outstripped the other. Giglamps George sat edgily at one end of a row, uneasy on his moulded plastic chair, while Spotter Jack sat further back, more confidently lounging, more at ease, convinced this time he'd done enough to take the precious title. "Now," said Mr Hepplethwaite, "we come to second place." A pregnant pause. "And once again, amazing as it seems, we have a tie..."

He might as well have said he was disqualified, or anything. A tie again! And after all that effort, all those evenings spent cross-checking, re-addressing, re-assessing. How on earth could Giglamps George have come within a million miles of such determined dedication? How? But George would never tell and, smiling, left the hall to cultivate enhancements of his own.

In fury then, we see our Jack fired with a missionary zeal and, blinded by defeat from any normal sense of rationality, pursuing in a single-minded manner his particular ambition—to ensure the second place for Giglamps George at next year's AGM.

So on the day the Vogons came, hiss-spitting with an ozone stench through heavy skies in interstellar battleships, while all the other earthlings ran for cover, scrambling to find their futile hiding places, Jack was out—book thus, pen so—eyes open, noting down with glee the colour, size, and ion-superdrive displacement of each Taurean cruiser, Sagittarian destroyer, Farside frigate, firing gigajoules of life-destroying, shelter-penetrating Z-rays into helpless humanoid enclosures.

Disinterested, and with his feelings focused on the job in hand as was his wont, Jack entered in his feint-lined book a technically precise review of all he saw, an eye-witness account of Armageddon, while he waited to collect the ultimate award, the undisputed scoop of this or any other century—the first, the very first non-human autograph to be acquired on Earth.

Then, when it all was done, the final item entered and the last dear detail noted in his ordered hand, Jack looked up, looked around—to find he was alone. No four-armed battle captain swaggering towards him down the ramp of victory, no multi-headed envoy of a distant world to greet him and his proffered pen. The ships had gone, and only smoking scarred-black sepulchres of past humanity waited to salute his return to reality.

The new custodian, sole survivor of a devastated planet; along with Grandpa Henshaw's khaki gas-mask case containing Thermos, sandwich box and camera—and, as before, the precious feint-lined, spiral-bound, hard-backed black notebook, filled with signatures in front and facts at back, for Spotter Jack to analyse and summarise and quantify and modify in the seclusion of his solitary evenings, solitary mornings, solitary night times, till his lonely dying day.

Batting Safe

I caught an outside edge—the merest snick of leather kissing willow. It should have been all over but, by great good fortune, keeper and first slip each thought the other had it covered. So, instead of losing me, we gained four precious runs. I can't believe it—me, the last man in, more ducks to my name than Donald, and I'm still at the crease.

But that's the problem. Should have got a single—let McGregor take the strike. Can't hope to be so lucky next time. Panic! One to draw, two to win—and only three balls left. Keep cool now. Stand up straight and stare around imperiously—pretend you're in control—look poised to place the next shot where they've left the gaps. What gaps? They've set the field so close you can almost smell what each one's had for lunch. Perhaps just there, through mid-off? Don't be silly, man, you'll never see it coming—far less worry where it goes.

I thought so, here comes Ron McGregor now—he's walking down the pitch to have a little word. Some fatherly advice, no doubt—though what he thinks he'll teach me in the space of fifteen seconds goodness knows. Yes, Ron, I'll play it safe—no, no more swipes—yes, fine, just push it up the pitch, and bloody run—OK, I understand. The theory's great—the trouble is, it's me that's got to do it. "Just needs confidence," he says, then gives me "Thumbs up mate," and plods his twenty paces back across the sacred turf.

I probe the ground in front of me, survey the square for pits and bumps and try to look intelligent. A bald patch here, a divot cut out there. Then suddenly, "Howzat!" I jump—how's what? They haven't stumped me while I wasn't watching, have they? Oh, I see—some joker in the field just caught the ball. They're lobbing it around to pass the time of day until the bowler's ready. Very funny! Gross intimidation, I should call it—what do *you* think, Umpire? Rats, he isn't looking—typical—he's from the other side. And now, what's this?—their captain's making signals—moving everyone even closer. Glory, weren't they near enough already, mate? I feel like piggy in the middle here—looks like the team could all shake hands around me. Only one gap left—it's right in front of me, straight up the wicket.

Has the bowler got that ball yet? Where's he gone? He can't have disappeared, but blessed if I can see him. Ah yes, there he is— involved in conversation with the skipper! Surely can't be much to talk about—just bang it down to me and take the off stump out, that's how it's generally done. Come on, get on with it.

But maybe those four runs have got them worried. Maybe he'll not bowl another fast one—far too risky. "Nice and slow," they'll say, "that way the batsman has to do the work. If we can make him swing his bat, we've got him." 'Spect they're right too—leave me standing here, bat raised, legs crossed, no bails and stumps akimbo. That's what I'd do anyway, if I were them—and I'm a bowler after all, so I should know.

They're still there, yakking on. It's gamesmanship—they want to make me nervous—give me time to think up all those stupid strokes tail-enders seem to make so easily. Well, two can play at that game. Let's just wait until he's ready, then... Ah, there he goes now, walking down to start his run. It looks like it's a long one too, to make me think he's going to bowl a scorcher I suppose. He's in no hurry either—strolling almost to the boundary. Perhaps he's going home for tea. No, here he comes. He turns and starts to move—so now it's time for me to say, "Excuse me, Umpire—give me middle and off, please?"

Out goes the Umpire's arm. I watch the bowler, caught in mid-stride, pull up awkwardly—the crouching circle round me rise as one—and testily, eleven pairs of eyes converge on me to wish me down in hell, or worse.

"To left, to left, to right—just there." I give the crease a few judicious thumps, "Thank you," and flash a friendly smile around the field—I'm ready now. They're not amused—their jaws are set, and I can see a look in every stony face which says, "You cocky little sod, you'll pay for this." Perhaps I will—but then maybe, now that my knees aren't knocking and I've made them all as sore as bears, perhaps I'll get the better of them yet.

The bowler's walking back again, and giving me a little glance from time to time to make sure I'm still ready. Look, no tricks—I'm calm, I'm waiting for you, do your worst. He frowns—he's got a worried sort of air about him—something in his stride seems less self-confident. I've got him rattled—or perhaps I'm just a life-long optimist.

Well here we go, it's now or never. After rubbing ball on buttock one more time, he starts again—a loping run, but not too fast—just as I thought. He doesn't want to give me anything to chip at. All the same, I know the man's no spinner of the ball, so if it's slow he'll have to keep it straight and pitch it where he thinks I'll have least chance to swipe at it. I can't move back and hit it on the rise—the stumps get in the way. I could go forward—try to whack it while it's in the air, before it hits the ground. But hang on, think about what Ron just said. He's not expecting me to win the match. "Just play it safe," he said, "and leave the winning shot to me." So be it, Ron, I'll stonewall at my crease for you and hope you've got your skates on.

Twenty strides—subconsciously I count them as he runs at me. Arm over wicket, front foot down and, with a grunt, he hurls his missile. Concentrate—that speck of black against the sight-screen, coming at you in a fixed parabola—it's meant for you, so keep your eye on it. I play the shot as if by rote—my left arm straight, my bat tipped slightly forward—textbook stuff, a classic stance, and—magically—I hear that nutty click as ball strikes bat plumb at the centre of percussion. Off it flies, and so do I—in reflex action—from my mark without a sideways glance, and making for the other crease like Linford Christie.

Visions of white shapes in motion all around me, then—I've made it! Turn round, see how Ron's got on. What's this?—he's waving, coming back. Good God, he's on a second run! I don't believe it—after all, I only gave the thing a gentle tap. So down the pitch I sprint again, and even faster this time. "Overthrow," Ron shouts out we cross. And so it was—I reach the crease again, we've won the match—and all off my shot, miracle of miracles.

I'd not seen how it happened, but Ron told me later—two men diving for my shot had hit their heads and knocked themselves unconscious. Then a third, in desperation, shied the ball towards the wicket, missed the stumps, found second slip and knocked him over too. The ball bounced off the poor man's head and ran away down to the off-side boundary. "We nearly made another four," said Ron, his dour face cracking with a hint of humour, "but why be extravagant when two will do the job?"

I grinned. "And did I play it safe enough?" I asked him with a twinkle in my eye.

He looked at me. "Aye, that you did," he said, "although I don't imagine three men in the other team will think so." And with that—I swear this is the truth, though no-one else who knows the man believes me—Ron McGregor took me to the bar and offered me a drink. Two miracles in one day!

"Thanks, Ron," I beamed—then on an impulse, throwing safety to the winds for once, I added, "Could I have a double?"

Away from the Coast

They said we had it 'cushy' where we were, twenty miles in from the coast. That's what the guys told me, the ones who'd been down there. Showing off their English slang, of course, like we all did. Well maybe it wasn't so bad here, but don't think we didn't suffer too, in our own way.

First thing we learnt when we got over here was that we'd moved into a war zone. Food rationed, gas masks to be carried and no lights at night. Still, we'd come for adventure, and this was it. We'd soon be away and pushing on over the Rhine, wherever that was. Give old Hitler a bloody nose, then back to the girls in Alberta with such stories to tell.

But months passed and we sat doing nothing. Well, not exactly nothing—there were courses and exercises and sports fixtures and parades and dances and tea parties and most nearly everything else put on to occupy our free time. And also there were the pubs—but that's a story I'd rather not go into here, us being greenhorns from the prairies and not familiar with the potent properties of warm mild and stout until it was too late!

We could see on the Pathé News that someone was fighting somewhere, but, as some joker put it, they had tanks and guns while we had bits of wood and the occasional jeep. The one thing that brought the 'real' war to us was scrambling for cover whenever the air raid siren sounded, and since this seemed to become a regular occurrence at about seven in the evening whether or not any enemy planes came over, we soon formed a plan to bivouac in the woods away from the base at night. Better to die in the open air than in some tin shed or dug-out pit of a shelter. The locals smiled indulgently, and agreed with each other that this was how Canadians were expected to behave—they'd seen it all before in the Wild West movies.

But one night I was caught out. Millie the local telephone operator was to blame. We'd been meeting now and then over the last few days, and I knew she worked the evening shift in a town exchange about five miles away. Eager to impress, I found some excuse to commandeer a delivery truck and made sure I was parked near her house when she came out with her bike that night. Took her by surprise, but she didn't show it—just gave me a wink and cycled off round the corner to wait for me to come by. I fairly hurled her bike into the back of the truck and pulled her up beside me in the cab—then we were off, driving to town by the scenic route.

It was that time of night when the Home Guard were turning out for their evening watch, and as we came up to one of their posts a white-haired gentleman with a neat military moustache stepped out in front of us and raised his arm. He informed me, in clipped tones, that he wouldn't advise me to use that route, if he were me, as they'd had warnings of German aircraft movements in our general direction, and this road passed right by the main army base. Prime target, didn't I know.

I knew. But I had a prime target of my own sitting right beside me, and a bird in the cab seemed to me to be worth more than several possible bomb craters in the bush at that moment. So we moved on, much to the gentleman's disapproval, claiming we had urgent business and no other possible way of getting there. Much good it did us. Two minutes later the siren went off, and a pair of MPs appeared from nowhere in the middle of the road, indicating in no uncertain manner that we should get out of that truck and under cover double quick.

The cover turned out to be an inspection pit in the workshop of a nearby garage. Millie and me would have fitted in just nicely, but unfortunately three greasy car mechanics were in there too. Give Millie her due, she didn't bat an eyelid—even seemed to enjoy it, which didn't please me none—and as for the garage guys, they thought Christmas had come early.

We were there a quarter of an hour—half an hour—it seemed like a lifetime. Four men and Millie pressed together like pilchards in a can, and still no 'all clear.' Any thrill there might have been in hoping for an illicit brush against buttoned bosom or serge-covered thigh had long since gone, and we were thankful when Millie finally declared that, bombs or no bombs, she had to get to her work—the war effort would suffer if nobody could make any telephone calls, wouldn't it. No doubt, we said—and gave her the most gentlemanly assistance in scrambling out of the pit.

Couldn't take her any further in the truck—one sound from that and the MPs would be back faster than you could say 'Provost Corps'—so we bid farewell to the mechanics and made for town on foot in the gathering twilight. I kept to the greensward so that my Size 12 army boots would make less noise. Just as well—those Red Caps were still on patrol, but we slipped by unnoticed. Even better, I found Millie's hand was gripping mine—not a bad night's effort so far, I thought. Could almost imagine myself walking down the aisle.

Then came the bang—well, we felt it more than heard it—and although it was a good fifty yards away, we found ourselves blown flat on our faces. A cluster of bombs fell, and each one shook the ground as we lay there. After the last, we didn't wait for the next lot—straight opposite us was a door in a solid-looking wall—no bones broken, we crossed the road faster than Jesse Owens, pushed the door open and bundled ourselves inside. Then we looked around, and slowly it dawned—we'd stumbled straight into the Red Caps' Officers' Mess. Out of the frying pan and into the proverbial fire.

And where were those brave khaki-clad sons of the Mounties? They were hiding under the billiard table, every one of them—and soon, we were under there with them.

This time we waited for the 'all clear.' I was out-ranked and off limits, but Millie worked her charm on them and I was let out with a caution, to find my own way back to the truck and my regiment. She was driven to work in a convoy of military jeeps—they said they were doing the trip to check up on bomb damage, but it seemed to me they took the wrong road for that. Anyway, Millie never needed a lift from me again—there was always an MP's vehicle outside her gate from then on.

On my way back, the same old gentleman from the Home Guard stopped me. I'd made it then, he said, and without any trouble? No trouble at all, I replied. The explosions had come from just about where he'd estimated me to have been, he said. He was worried about the young filly—was she safe? I gave him a slow prairie stare. Depends on what you mean by safe. The Germans didn't get her, I said, and left it at that.

He told me that an old lady had run back to her house after the siren went, to fetch her canary, and got a direct hit. She'd been the only one killed this time, as far as he was aware. Nice old girl too, he knew the family. I told him I was sorry, and drove on through the dark lanes to find where the rest of the boys had camped that night. Millie, I thought, could have been my canary. Better for me to stay safely in the bushes at night than have that bird in my hand.

And so I did, and watched the moon sailing through the pines and thought how funny that it looked the same as back home. And thought, too, how peaceful it all was when there was supposed to be a war on.

Then just two weeks later they found us some tanks, and soon after that they moved us south. Joe Stalin wanted to see some action on the Western front, and Winnie knew that us Canadians were just sitting here twiddling our fingers, so he organised an expedition for us—to Dieppe and back. Except not many came back. And those that did knew then, if they hadn't known before—how cushy it was away from the coast.

Shortlisted by 'Writers News', February 1997

Juno Beach and Beyond

On the 50th anniversary of D-Day, I was privileged to introduce a Canadian veteran to a class of 14-year olds at a local school. They asked him some direct questions, and he gave them direct answers. These are largely his words.

Fresh-faced fourteen,
beautiful children,
boisterous scholars,
with freedom to talk and argue,
make their point,
and put their hats on back to front,
in England, 1994.

That's why we fought
and many big men cried
on Juno Beach
and through the weeks beyond.

"And did you hate the Germans?"
Fifty years ago, we had a job to do,
a Bully, if you like, to put in place,
and men like us, but dressed in grey
had their job too.

We didn't know
of Belsen, Auschwitz and the rest;
not then. Perhaps, who knows,
if we'd known half the truth
we farmers from the prairies,
loggers from the seaboard,
might have hated more
the conscripts
from the hamlets of the fatherland
who traded shots with us
among the stinking orchards
there in Normandy.

But as it was,
we had a job to do,
a worth-while job,
and did it to our best.

"How old were you?"
Eighteen, and scared
of never seeing nineteen,
never having all the good things
life had promised, scared of dying,
but, above all,
scared of showing I was scared.

Just eighteen, volunteered at sixteen,
anxious then to see the world,
and found my future led across the bar
of Juno Beach.

Eighteen, but we were men
compared with some of those in grey–
young boys, by-products of a system:
fresh-faced fourteen,
beautiful children,
earnest students,
with no freedom to talk or argue,
make their point,
or put their hats on back to front
like you in England now.

So let me look at you again,
your cheeky grins,
your mischievous ways;
and let me remember
the reason why—
it was all for you,
and your smiling eyes
that we soldiered on
and comrades died
on Juno Beach and beyond.

Winding Point

I'd done it without thinking. As soon as I read that note on the table, I'd run for cover. Spontaneous reaction. Familiar territory—my territory—and all the seclusion I needed.

And I did need seclusion. No nosy neighbours to offer me their ritual sympathy in return for the chance of some juicy gossip. Sheila was gone — how should I react? Funny. Even at that moment, I was more concerned about how I should look to the outside world than how I should cope without her. Pride, I suppose, plus a typical Englishman's reserve.

Burbage was on the water at her summer moorings. Three hours later I was at her helm, weekend case stowed below, and the sedge grass dipping and rising to my passage down the cut. With the throttle at tickover, life slowed down to a walking pace. Time to ponder. Time to think of an answer. Time to...

Four miles an hour is not fast, but bends and blind bridges can come upon you suddenly on a canal. Though I knew this stretch well, my mind was elsewhere, and the prow appearing through the narrow brick arch ahead caught me unawares. I threw the engine hard into reverse, and predictably began to veer across the channel. When the other helmsman caught sight of me some five seconds later, I was pretty well touching both banks at once.

Burbage is made of quarter-inch steel plate up to cabin level, reinforced with steel rubbing bars fore and aft. She is designed for a rough life, and canal work is never a contact-free operation. But to have her struck amidships with a similarly solid bow and the momentum of seventy-two feet of steel plate behind it — this was not something I wished to witness, far less participate in. Dear reader, at that moment I prayed — and the God of travellers and fishermen, or whoever was on duty that day, saw to it that the smallest of gaps opened up between *Burbage* and the bank. The oncoming boat found its way through this and did a slow motion 'wall of death' climb onto the muddy shallows. There was much revving of engine and levering with barge-poles until it slid slowly back into the deeper water behind me and carried on its way, leaving the water brown and turbulent with excitement. And not a word was spoken between the crews.

This, I reflected, was the aspect of canal boating not mentioned in the brochures. Lose concentration at the helm, and four miles an hour seems like seventy. Perhaps that was why Sheila would never... I stopped short in my thoughts. Sheila.

What had the note said? In my rush to be away I'd left it behind. 'Arrogant' was a word that sprang to mind. She found me arrogant. Me. That was the last thing I was. What about her — always wanting her own way? Where did we go on holidays? — where she wanted. Where did we go to eat? — where she wanted. Where did we...? Well, yes, that too — where and when she wanted. How come it was me that was arrogant then?

'Uncaring' too. Same thing, I suppose. Arrogant means uncaring, doesn't it? Well, near as. 'Arrogant and uncaring.' Doesn't that simply mean I like to get my own way from time to time? Don't we all? We can't all be 'arrogant and uncaring' just because we like to have it our own way on occasions. Must be more to it than that.

The fishermen lining the bank raised their rods one after the other in sullen salute as *Burbage* passed by, then re-baited the water and cast again until the next uncaring boater might arrive to spoil their idyll. We were sharing the same water, both with the best of motives, but each with different objectives. Rather like life in general, really. Relationships—partnerships—differences of opinion—compromise —tolerance. Sheila...

I found myself returning quickly to the 'here and now' as the first lock appeared round a bend in the distance, white balance beams reflected in still water, and a cluster of craft moored along the towpath below. It says something about my state of mind. Experienced canal-user that I was, I hadn't thought of the problem of locking single-handed until then. 'Jump on the boat, run it up and down the canal a bit until I feel I've sorted myself out, then go back home'—if I'd had a plan at all, that would just about express it. A solitary coming to terms with... whatever it was that had to be come to terms with. But operating a lock was different—it had always been a joint effort.

As we'd approach, perhaps from a quarter of a mile or so away, Sheila would jump on shore with the handle and run ahead to prepare the chamber. I always tried to slow the boat down so I could steer straight in through the open gates without mooring. She'd close the gates behind me and open up the sluices, while I played around with the engine to keep *Burbage* clear of sills and ledges until the water found its new level. Then as gates opened in front of me, I'd emerge slowly for her to jump on board again, and we'd head off towards pastures new, and probably thoughts of lunch at the next pub.

I was quarter of a mile away now, and no Sheila. I tried to remember where I'd put the mooring spikes and mallet—it would be just my luck to find no rings on the bank here—and I hoped I'd stowed the ropes neatly enough to be able to get at them quickly. There was a breeze blowing off the towpath shore too, and I'd rather not end up with *Burbage* wedged across the cut again.

It was a long three minutes. The black gate came nearer and I began to search for a space to pull in. There was less room than I'd have liked, and in the end I had to make do with a gap between two moored boats where the towpath had fallen away. Slowly I edged the nose to the bank, then pushed the tiller hard over to bring the stern in. Nothing doing. It was obvious now why nobody else was there—too shallow. I'd have to try again further up. Select reverse. Still nothing doing—I was stuck.

Now the art of using the proverbial ten-foot barge-pole to lever a boat off mud is not too difficult, provided you have a firm footing on the boat and a reasonably solid bank on which to push. I had both of these, and with a only modicum of grinding *Burbage* began to move sideways into deeper water. Unfortunately, this happened to coincide with the sudden opening of the lock gate sluices for a boat coming down, and before I knew it I was effectively white-water rafting across the canal at an unseemly rate.

My first thought was to get back to the controls with all speed, my second was to wish goodbye to the barge pole as it dropped into the maelstrom in my haste, and my third was to curse my mobile phone for starting to ring now of all times. The sound of china smashing in the galley below indicated that we had made the equivalent of an emergency stop—in this case against the opposite bank. I had braced myself, but even so found one or other of Newton's laws was determined to demonstrate itself by hurling me into the water.

The phone was still chirruping as I waded round the hull of the now beached *Burbage*, up to my waist in green slime and puddle clay, and dragged myself up through a crop of luxuriant nettles to lie on the dry earth beyond. I reached in my jacket to see who was calling. As I did so, the cause of my predicament emerged from the lock. I answered the phone just as the name of the boat came into view—*Sheila*.

"Pardon?"

"It's Sheila. Look—I said I'm sorry."

"You're…"

"Will you be coming home now?"

It so happened that the point on the canal where I'd been washed up was wide enough to turn a boat the length of *Burbage*—a winding point in fact. I stretched out on my back and suddenly the world was wonderful.

"Yes, I'm coming home just as fast as *Burbage* can make base."

"*Burbage*? You're on *Burbage*?"

I'd forgotten, of course, that she hadn't known where in the world I was. "Well not exactly *on* her at the moment, but we're by the first lock and…"

"Don't move then—I'm coming to you!"

So she came to me, at the winding point. And later that evening, at a more isolated mooring, *Burbage* rocked to the gentle rhythm of reconciliation.

And you want a moral to this story? Sorry—apparently I'm still too uncaring and arrogant to be interested. Go fish for a ten-foot barge-pole!

Shortlisted by 'Writers News', April 1997

Crime Doesn't Pay

"Listen, they say crime doesn't pay. Maybe it doesn't. Or maybe it does, but it doesn't pay enough."

"Can we go on now?"

"You listening to me? This is important."

"No kidding!"

"What's crime anyway? I mean, who says a crime is a crime?"

"The Government. Now are we…"

"You said it—the Government—the biggest load of crooks around."

"What *is* this?"

"Now if a crook says something's a crime, who are we to believe?"

"Jesus!"

"Treason must fail—pray tell me the reason?
For if it succeeds, none dare call it treason."

"If I want a lesson in English literature…"

"The only real crime is getting caught. And if you've done something big enough, nobody *wants* to catch you—or even admit you've done it."

"Please."

"If enough important people depend on what you've done…"

"I get the message, now can we just get on?"

"Am I touching a raw nerve?"

"I said let's get on."

"Why should I get on—because *you* say so?"

"You know why."

"I know why *you* think why. Maybe I think different."

"So?"

"You don't think it's important what I think?"

"Right now—no."

"Just because I'm—you know—you think that means I don't have anything worth saying?"

"Oh, you've things worth saying alright."

"I have too."

In the next room, a trainee deputy under-secretary's assistant's clerk turned off the light to go home.

"You know what I think?"

"What's this?"

"D'you want to know what I think?"

"I'm asking the questions here."

"Were you?"

"You're guilty, and I'm asking the questions."

"Why ask then, if I'm guilty?"

"We need evidence."

"Of?"

"Your crime."

"Which is?"

"I'm asking the questions."

"Nonsense."

"How much?"

"In round figures?"

"Exactly."

"About…"

"Exactly."

"… five times the figure you're thinking of."

"Some smart Alec, eh?"

"No laughing matter."

"We're wasting time."

"Your time, not mine."

"Not yet. Only a matter of time though, before it is—so to speak."

"Is this an interrogation?"

"Interesting word that—interrogation."

"Why's that?"

"Has implications."

She was waiting at the bus-stop when he was driven past in a black limousine. But it didn't mean that he was happier than she was.

"You were saying?"

"Nothing important."

"We could make the cost unacceptable."
"To whom?"
"Somebody pays in the end."
"Always the next in line."
"There has to be an end."
"If the Chinese marched past six abreast there'd never be an end."
"Perpetual laundering?"
"No crime there."
"And no pay either."
"But you…"
"I'm the only one marching in step. Metaphorically."
"And reaping rewards."
"*The rain it raineth all the time*
 Upon the just and unjust fellah,
 But mainly on the just because
 The unjust's just snitched his umbrella."
"Remind me to cancel your poetic licence."
"Not in your gift. God-given."
"God-dammit, you wriggle more than a garter snake."
"I learnt my trade in the Garden of Eden. An apple a day…"
"Who's in charge here?"
"You asking me?"
"No, the wallpaper."
"Thought you might be getting rhetorical. You are."
"You're kidding me!"
"No. I've no ambition to be in charge here, so you must be."
"Well then, since I'm in charge—and thank you kindly…"
"Don't mention it."
"… Perhaps I can hope for a bit of co-operation now."

Instant coffee doesn't have quite the same glamour as the real thing, especially when made in a stained and chipped Snoopy mug. But you can mix it as strong or as weak as you like—and you don't have to get rid of the grounds like he does. The grounds…

"How long have you been involved in all this?"
"I don't answer questions from you—you answer them from me."
"Ah, you're playing white then."
"Who?"
"Chess. White leads. I'm black."
"Don't tempt me with a relevance."
"Make your move then."
"This is no game. If you're found guilty…"

"I'm guilty—you said so, remember?"
"It's possible."
"You *said* it."
"Jes-*us*."
"So, if I'm found guilty…"
"You're guilty."
"Again."
"You're guilty…"
"Bless you."
"… As I stand here."
"… And covered in glory…"
"Your glory's just hit the fan."
"Your fan or mine?"
"I don't have fans—just superiors and turkeys. Shut up and listen to me for a moment, won't you?"
"My lips are sealed."
"We know you did it, we know when you did it, and we know how you did it—right? I said, right? All we want to know now is who you did it with and where you put it—OK? I said, OK? Speak to me will you!
"You told me to shut up and listen."
"Mercy, may the tape record the provocation—and still I did not strike the client."

A night at the opera is beyond the reach of a trainee deputy under-secretary's assistant's clerk. But she may listen to a tape recording, and dream that she's there with him, in the box.

"Not a night for answers."
"You again?"
"It seems I'm needed here."
"Who by? Not by me."
"Just needed—passive tense."
"But on active service."
"Civil perhaps. Are you ready to begin?"
"We began long ago."
"A false start I believe."
"Believe what you like—we began."
"But to no purpose."
"If you say so…"
"I do."
"… then you'd better make it clear what you want."
"Follow the rules."

"They've changed them since I was at school."
"Improvements."
"Changes."
"Let's not dispute their judgement."
"Ha! But *we* aren't both in the same situation."
"The rules…"
"Are the rules are the rules."
"If everybody broke the rules…"
"Everybody breaks the rules."
"Your perspective, not mine."
"Mediaeval."
"Now what?"
"Your perspective. Unreal, no vanishing point."

Bed can come as a relief or as a frustration. He is not always the man for the occasion, and she may not (might not?, must not?) be a failure. Records may be changed, but never in her favour.

"I'll tell you where it's gone."
    "Do, please."
    "To a third party."
    "Party? You could be right."
    "Pulling the strings—your strings."
    "That sort of party!"
    "Got form on you."
    "You have?"
    "No, he has."
    "Funny. Third party?—who's the second?"
    "Manner of speaking. Who is he?"
    "Santa Claus."
    "We could be on your side."
    "On my back you mean."
    "Offer protection."
    "Mates all round?"
    "It's a serious offer."
    "Sounds more like a proposition to me."
    "Unlikely, don't you think?"
    "I'm not paid to think."
    "The man."
    "The third man?"
    "Party."
    "What's it worth?"
    "You're not paid to think. Just tell."

"That wasn't thinking—that was reflex."
"Knee jerk."
"Jerk—you're getting warm."
"Pardon?"
"A pain in groin."
"You've lost me."
"Mr Big—or thinks he is. Your third bleedin' party."

Morning is parturition and partition—the bringing forth and the separation—the present given for the past in expectation of the future. Morning is a daily mourning of muddled experiences and missed opportunities.

"Wages of sin."
    "Can be substantial."
    "Not with Johnny—just a retainer—a tip for a job well done."
    "Was it?"
    "What?"
    "Well done."
    "Depends which job you mean."
    "I mean…"
    "I know what you mean. Yes, it was well done—and so was the other thing."
    "And the other thing was all you got."
    "All I ever got. All I ever get."
    "I'm sorry."
    "You'll need me at the trial? Should be big in the *Sun*."
    "There'll be no trial, and no interviews. Official Secrets."
    "Hushed up? He's getting away with it?"
    "Measures will be taken."
    "What measures."
    "Adequate measures. He'll not profit by it."
    "Nor me."
    "Nor you. Good luck in the new job."
    "New job?"
    "In the best interests of all. You'll be offered a transfer of course—north west Scotland I believe—but I doubt if you'll be interested."
    "But I…"
    "You're free to go now."
    "Free?"
    "Completely. Here's money for the bus fare home."
    "So crime does pay—three quid and on the dole."

"Keep the change."

The panelled door closed solidly behind him, and in the next room a trainee deputy under-secretary's assistant's clerk turned off the light to go home. Unconnected except by time and location, they walked together to the bus stop, silent in their own private thoughts.

Wild Dogs

(a cautionary Pantoum)

A hound as you know can run wild in a pack,
Whenever you slip off the lead you should care,
And once he's away he may never come back,
It just takes a small thing to make him go spare.

Whenever you slip off the lead you should care,
He could be in sheep and he could be in trouble,
It just takes a small thing to make him go spare,
And he'll be away in a trice at the double.

He could be in sheep and he could be in trouble,
Once out of your sight he'll be out of control,
And he'll be away in a trice at the double
On seeing a rabbit run into its hole.

Once out of your sight he'll be out of control,
There's no way for you to speed up his return,
On seeing a rabbit run into its hole,
He'll take off like Concorde with full afterburn.

There's no way for you to speed up his return,
A hound as you know can run wild in a pack,
He'll take off like Concorde with full afterburn,
And once he's away he may never come back.

Published in 'The Countryman', February 1992

Deep Wells

When Jane Jackson's kitten fell down the old well in the garden of her Victorian house, she knew immediately how to get it out again.

Lowering the mewing mother on a makeshift sling, she correctly predicted that maternal instinct would overcome fear, the cat would grab the neck of its waterlogged offspring in her mouth, and mother and daughter would be hauled together safely back to the surface, and to a vigorous rubbing with towels.

And some time later she received a commendation from an animal welfare organisation who had heard about the event and decided to honour the quick-witted owner. Quick-witted, yes—today we might say that she used lateral thinking—but she had good reason to remember. After all, her own mother had once…

* * *

"Jane, your father's gone." Her mother had the habit of making a crisis out of a mishap, so Jane took little notice of the ritual trespass in her room and pointedly carried on reading her book as if nothing had happened.

"Jane?"

Established procedure now demanded that she lift her eyes slowly from her book, and aim a pained expression in her mother's direction. She did this.

"Did you hear me? He's gone!"

"I heard you, mother." Her eyes drifted back to the book; she was in the middle of an interesting bit.

"Gone! How can you sit there?" Her mother made her customary dash across the room, and when she was within striking distance Jane, as usual, snapped the book shut and moved it out of reach. For a few silent seconds mother and daughter looked each other in the eye, daring one another to blink, to breathe, to utter the next word.

Her mother broke first: "You don't care about anyone but yourself, do you?"

"Moth-*er*." The scene ran on as predictably as a play script. Pretence of catastrophe from mother; pretence of disinterest from daughter; both reciting old, worn lines, and both succeeding only in tracing yet one more groove in the record of failed empathy. Then, suddenly, the needle jumped; the script changed.

"Jane, I need your help." Her mother was earnest.

Flummoxed as an actor who had been fed a wrong cue in a familiar passage, Jane's mind raced for the right reply. Slowly, carefully, playing for time, "Moth-*er*," she repeated.

"I need your help."

The tone had an edge to it which Jane had not heard before. Tonight they were using new material. Improvising now, she replied, "Why, what's wrong?" She was letting slip an admission that her mother might for once have a real problem; exposing a dangerous chink in her emotional armour which her mother could prise open.

But the reply was muted. "Come with me—I have to show you."

"Show what?"

"Downstairs—please. Come."

"But I'm..." Jane stopped in mid-sentence; the normal conventions had been broken, and the normal responses no longer seemed appropriate. Grudgingly, "Oh, all *right*."

They came down the open staircase into the lounge, mother and daughter. And there below, sitting in the armchair by the window, Jane saw her father—apparently asleep. She stopped, involuntarily clutching her mother's arm, fearing the worst.

"I thought you said..."

"His body's there, but he's not..." Her mother's whisper faltered; she unhitched Jane's hand from her arm and continued downstairs. Jane followed, curious and anxious in equal measures, tiptoeing over to the chair where her mother was already in conversation with the body.

"Jack? Jack, can you hear me? It's Agnes, Jack."

"Is he...?"

"Dead? Oh no, he's just gone away for a while—again."

"Again?"

Her mother put a hand on his forehead and then knelt on the floor beside the chair to feel his pulse. She remained motionless in this position for a minute, then gave a nod of satisfaction. "It happens, or at least it used to, from time to time. Not so often lately—I thought he'd stopped doing it."

"He—comes back, does he?"

"Always has so far." Her mother seemed to have pulled herself together, and stood up suddenly. "I must fetch your aunt—stay with him while I'm away, will you?"

Jane hesitated. "But what if he…"

But she was talking to no-one. The back door slammed shut and she heard her mother's receding footsteps on the gravel path. Tentatively, on her knees, she reached forward and touched her father's hand. It was warm. On an instinct, she gripped both his hands tightly and looked up at his face. His eyes were open, and there was an expression of serenity…

"Daddy," she whispered, "where are you?"

No sound, no movement. And yet, she heard—felt—a soft reply in her mind, in her imagination perhaps. It seemed to come from above her, or was it from behind? Or maybe—it was all around her, within her.

Frightened, she dropped his hands and prepared to run off; then she sensed, "Don't go." It was a request, not an order. Unspoken, but somehow received by her, and strangely comforting.

"Come to me, Jane." She reached out and took his hands again. This time they were more than just warm—they were alive, in an indescribable way. Tingling, almost. Not a sound in the room and yet, distinctly, "Come to me." She looked around her, half expecting to see a floating apparition speaking the words. Nothing. She turned back to look at her father—resting in peace, it seemed, in the armchair.

"Daddy," she whispered again, "how?"

* * *

Down the road, breathless from hurrying, her mother knocked at Aunt Maud's front door. "Come on, woman," she muttered to herself and knocked again, looking through the lace curtains for signs of life. A crack of light appeared from within, as the old spinster emerged from the kitchen and started to shuffle slowly along the hall. "Who is it?" piped a reedy voice.

"It's Agnes."

There was a fumbling of chains and the click of two dead-locks, then the slow opening of the door, and a gaunt stick of a woman stood there, challenging the world to cross her threshold. Even Agnes in her desperation didn't dare make a forward move until invited. Aunt

Maud inspected her with sharp eyes for what seemed an unnecessarily long time, then: "You'd better come in," she said.

Agnes was shepherded into the drawing room, for Aunt Maud would not receive even family in the kitchen. It was a cold, clean, spotlessly uncomfortable room. Aunt Maud perched on one of a pair of low-backed damask armchairs, and Agnes placed herself uneasily in the other, bursting with the news. But Aunt Maud spoke first, unbidden.

"So—you've got a problem, have you?"

* * *

Back up the road, Jane had no problem. She sat cross-legged on the floor beside her father's chair, eyes open and a peaceful expression on her face. From a distant viewpoint floating high above the house, yet seeing everything in perfect detail, she watched her father's body stir, stand up, inspect the form on the floor beside him, and walk out of the room. She followed him as he also made the journey down to Aunt Maud's house, to meet his wife just as she came out of the door.

"Jack?" For a moment she couldn't believe her eyes. Then anxiously, "Where's Jane?"

"Jane? She's fine." He'd avoided answering the question. Agnes was immediately suspicious.

"*Where*, Jack?"

"I left her in the lounge." By this time Aunt Maud had come to join them on the doorstep. She gave Jack a piercing look, and grunted. "Back already? That didn't last long."

Agnes ignored her and persisted; "You didn't *use* Jane did you? To get back?"

"She called me."

Jane looked down and felt she was there, standing right by them. "So that's what happened," she thought calmly.

"She brought you back before your time," Aunt Maud said sharply. "Now we're in a pickle."

"I feel fine."

"*You* might feel fine, Jack Jackson; I was thinking about that daughter of yours."

Agnes turned to her abruptly. "Is she in danger, Aunt Maud?"

Jane drifted lazily away from the scene and up, gliding as if on the wind. She felt perfectly relaxed, floating downstream in the sun, remembering times stretched out on the cushions of a rowing boat in the country. Danger? What could they mean?

"In danger? She could be," said Maud. "We must go back—to your house. Where's my coat?"

It was a warm day, but Aunt Maud was never seen outside without her coat and hat on. Urgent as she felt this mission might be, today was no exception. When she was suitably clad, the trio made its way back up the hill. Jane watched from her vantage point, detached and disinterested, as they entered the lounge and found the calm, unmoving figure squatting beside the chair. A figure which, Jane was only dimly aware, had something to do with her.

Her mother went to shake the body. "Don't touch her!" Aunt Maud snapped, "or we may lose her."

Agnes recoiled as if bitten. "Lose her? But *Jack* has always…"

"Jack comes back in his own good time—usually. There are protocols to be observed."

"Do we just leave her there—like that?" Agnes asked.

"Protocols," repeated Aunt Maud with finality.

Meanwhile Jane had drifted far away, and was beginning to wonder for the first time where she was, and how she had got there, and… Suddenly she realised it was all impossible. With the panic of a novice swimmer out of his depth for the first time, she struck out wildly; but with no physical body, this took the form of creating waves in an entirely different plane.

"She's thrashing," said Jack in a matter-of-fact voice, "I can feel it."

Aunt Maud, busy inspecting Jane's passive body, said nothing.

"How do we get her back?" Agnes was becoming more desperate by the minute, and found the calm, detached attitude of the other two almost too much to bear. "Jack? Maud? Can't we *do* something?"

Maud finished her inspection. "Yes, we can do something—*you* can do something."

Drowning—this is what drowning must feel like. Jane found her thoughts slipping, one over the other, as in a dream, as if in…

Agnes was seated in the armchair which her husband had so recently occupied. But now he stood on one side of her, facing her, holding her left hand, while Aunt Maud stood opposite, equally sternly, holding the other. 'Going fishing', they had said. She was the bait, and they were casting the line. Not into water, but into a far deeper stream, an infinite pool. A heartbeat from eternity.

Nothing is new. Everything we understand, and everything we have yet to understand, is built of variations on a common theme. Only circumstances change; the combination of countless small events which taken together display endless permutations and defy analysis.

Launched into the unearthly lake, doubly secured by the physical and mental constraints imposed by Jack and Maud, and guided by barely-felt forces, Agnes swam unerringly towards her child. Jane's memory afterwards was of a warm wave engulfing her, lifting her, and carrying her back to safety, to reality, to life.

* * *

"There you are, you silly thing—all dry now. You'll know better than to do that another time, won't you." The kitten skittered away across the room to attack the leg of a chair; the mother coiled herself on the rug and began, inevitably, to wash; and Jane, remembering another day when she herself had been pulled back just in time, took the last cigarette from her packet—and tried to relax again.

The Alice Effect

Have you ever wondered why mirrors reverse left to right, but never top to bottom? Lewis Carol almost got it right—almost but not quite, for the truth is far stranger than even he imagined it to be. That reflection you see of yourself—it's not looking at you, it's looking away from you. It has no front or back, being two-dimensional, but it still has a left and a right, an up and a down—and they are all in the same direction as your own.

I say 'it' has no front or back, but I would be more accurate to say 'he' or 'she,' for these are no mere lifeless objects which we see reflected before us. Quicksilver was aptly named—it gives life to a world which we can never inhabit—where time is the third dimension, not the fourth.

You think I jest? But I can prove it—and seven years' bad luck to you if you disbelieve me. First you must trust me—trust me to take you in spirit where your body cannot go. Do you? Then find a glass and look more closely upon your own reflection than you have done before. Go on, gaze at it—deeper and more intently than that. Let your eyes relax and lose their focus. Can it be yourself that's looking back? Surely not, for you are here and it is there. A reasonable likeness, to be sure, but there's something amiss—something not quite right. On reflection, it's just a poor mimic, a mere caricature of yourself.

* * *

The eyes are not yours. They look weary, and yours sparkle with energy.

Is that better?

Much better. You must learn to react more swiftly to the mood of the subject. You felt the unease?

Strongly.

He noticed your lapse. Concentrate on the waves—let them guide you. We are a dimension ahead, and we sense them before he does. But he is not an easy subject, this one.

He is about to look away.

Then move as he does. That's right. You're learning fast.

* * *

You noticed the eyes? I too. It's usually the eyes that give them away—I've seen that before. For one thing, we look at a person's eyes first; for another, they change without us thinking about it, a reflex action—bright lights will do it—and as it's our thoughts that they pick up, without those, they cannot operate.

Ah, but who are *they*? Yes indeed. Truth is sometimes stranger than we can imagine, or perhaps stranger than we wish to imagine. They feed on our thoughts—they are in fact, quite literally, the reflection of our imagination. Without us, they could not exist. They are parasites in a way—benign parasites to be sure, but parasites none the less. You shake your head in disbelief—but you saw for yourself. You want further proof? Very well, you shall have it.

* * *

He approaches.

Not physically.

His mind approaches—his body stays behind.

He is testing us. It happens sometimes—not often.

His mind separates from the physical form. Is this what they call dreaming?

No, it's different. In dreaming they are unaware of us—but this is more—a conscious challenge. Unusual.

And your advice?

Go to meet him.

* * *

You feel them tracking your mind? They lay their snares well. You will find your thoughts taking circular paths—bringing you back always to your point of departure. Always a reflection of your original thought, or so it seems. Perhaps more accurately a refraction, through many internal angles. Such things are their stock in trade.

But now you must break their hold. Strong will is not the answer—it would simply be returned to you amplified. No, you must starve them—starve them of thought while retaining your consciousness. A parasite cannot live without its source of food. Take control on your own terms, but gently. You fish? Well then, use your knowledge of the river—here you have a very large fish to be landed, but use no force—no force at all.

* * *

He fades. Is he receding?
    I cannot tell you—only one of us at a time may reflect with him.
    You are my mentor.
    I advise—I do not control. Trust your own judgement.
    I am learning. But you tell me this is not normal.
    Concentrate—do not lose him for an instant.
    Have I the right to refocus?
    On what?
    He becomes obscure.
    You make no sense. Explain.
    He merges with his own shadow. Have I the right to refocus there?
    You cannot. Shadows have no thoughts. Preview his intentions immediately.
    He has none.
    This is sheer madness! What are you doing?

* * *

No force at all—take it easy now. Your line must drift towards the prey. Think nothing, do nothing, be nothing. They will come to you. Not in body, for they have none, but in mind they will come to you. They have need. Stay quiet—they come, they come. Across the abyss from their quicksilver world to ours beyond. Projecting, prodding, probing—can you not feel them trying to penetrate your spirit? The only bridge they can construct. Intangible gossamer—yet strong as... You feel it now, do you not? But do not react to them— make no signal. Remember we are here to observe only, not to partake.

* * *

His mind is shut tight. I have lost him.

50

This is not possible. Never in all my aeons have I found a mind closed so tight that it cannot be prised open with skill. Give me the permit.

But protocol forbids…

Give, and do not argue—there is no space in our third dimension for argument.

Then I have failed?

We shall see—all is not lost. The permit!

* * *

Now do you believe? You doubted me at first, but feel the proof. This is no daydream—I have been here before and I know. Once, long ago—I was almost too young to remember—once they nearly caught me. There was a struggle, and it took willpower to tear myself away. Since then I've learnt to be more careful, more circumspect in my approach—and so must you. There are forces operating here which we cannot yet understand—intelligent forces.

It's time to leave them now. I've made my point, I think, have I not? But you look unconvinced. Why, what's the matter?

* * *

See, he comes. We have control now. You saw how I did it? Pay attention, or you'll never learn. I said, did you see how I did it?

Where am I?

For Dimension's sake, where do you think you are? Are you following me or not?

I can't move. I can't breathe.

And I'm losing my patience. Here, take the permit back and do it yourself.

I was out there looking in, and now…

Who are you?

Thin. Less than paper thin—how can this be?

Less than…? Aeons alive, dear mortal! You have been transferred. And you have lost a dimension in the process.

* * *

Heavy? You are feeling heavy? Strange—I've never found that effect. A little light-headed perhaps, but… but my dear fellow, what's wrong? You're folding up. Is your back broken? Here, let me help you. What's the problem? Lean on me—you seem unable to

51

support your own weight suddenly. And those eyes—they're not your eyes. Not your eyes at all. They're the eyes we saw in the…

* * *

He must smash the glass to release you. We cannot do it—it requires mass, and we have none.

Will he know that?

He may, if he stops to think of it. His thoughts at this moment are not logical.

Can we help him?

That is doubtful. He will have to come to his senses first.

Then I am trapped.

* * *

What are you? A spirit come to haunt us? What have you done to my friend? Where is he? Will you not answer me? What is your part in all this? Why will you not speak? Stand up, damn you! Look me in the eye and tell me. You are not my friend. Where is he? Will you not say?

Very well—I shall force it from you. If it takes murder, I shall force it from you. Don't try to act as though you're dead already—I'll make you speak. Stand up! Up! You won't? Then I'll pull you up—by your collar if necessary—and give you a good belt where it hurts while I'm at it—then we'll see who can't speak. Up I said! Use you legs—no? Right then, you asked for it!

* * *

He comes.

He's nowhere near.

Trust me, he comes. His future is my present. A fight, a blow, a mass in movement. Your body.

My body? Here?

Very soon. And then the glass will break. Farewell.

* * *

Let me get you a bandage—it's not a deep cut. Just missed the jugular. Another half inch that way and it would have been a different story. Look at the shards on the floor—some no bigger than a pencil. And each one its own small mirror. A single reflection has become many—and within each new reflection…

Within each new reflection, there is a new world.

The Beautiful Game

The way I see it,
Brian,
at the end of the day,
Life's a game of two halves.

First you go out there all fresh,
eager to make your mark,
please the crowd,
show off your ball skills—know what I mean?
Get stuck into the opposition,
score with a few,
try not to pick up too many yellow cards.

Then comes the turn-round—half time—
married,
get a lecture from the boss
on tactics, and especially
ball control.

Second half—different game—
you've one or two in the net yourself,
so no more thoughts of scoring now,
don't argue with the ref,
protect your goal,
and keep that work-rate up.
You've got to feed the others,
move the action up to them—
it's their turn now
to try and sneak one in.

And at the final whistle,
when you leave that pitch,
Brian,
you hope the manager has seen enough
to keep your name on his list
and pick you for the team next week.
You know what I mean?

It's a funny old game, Life.

First published in 'Weyfarers', Issue 76, 1996

That's what Friends are for

"Dr and Mrs A.P. Garrett have great pleasure in…"

Arthur held on to the card for a moment more, as if letting go would be an act of betrayal. Then he laid it carefully on top of the pile of scrawled notes, old receipts, and other miscellaneous items which Eileen had kept in her bottom drawer. *Had* kept.

Tomorrow it would be a week. Seven days since he had come downstairs from the study, thinking it must be about teatime, to find Eileen asleep, as he thought, in her chair. "Slipped away quietly," the doctor had said; "Wish we could all go like that." And suddenly Arthur had realised that, for the first time in his life, he was quite alone in the world.

During the next few days he had gone through cycles of bewilderment, panic and disbelief, as shadowy bodies came and went, and the physical Eileen, truly his 'better half' for more than forty years, disappeared from his life for ever. Only now could he begin to come to terms with the reality of his new situation, starting with a determination to remember their best times together, but not hang on to every last scrap of a memory.

With a sigh he sat back and rubbed his spine. Eileen would be telling him to get up and do something else for a while, and making him a cup of tea. Well, he was quite capable of making tea himself. Standing up slowly, he stretched and made his way towards the kitchen. Time—that was the villain of the piece and also the saviour. Time to reflect despondently on what might have been, or time to live the rest of life to the full, the choice was his. Eileen had not been one to be over-sentimental; he could almost hear her saying, "Get on and publish that research material you've been collecting all these years. You've got the time now."

A knock at the front door brought him suddenly out of his daydream.

"Hello, I do hope you don't mind me calling." It was Mrs Wearing, aptly named Arthur thought, who lived across the road and was one of Eileen's small circle of friends. "I just thought I'd come and see if you're alright—whether I can do anything for you." A smile flickered uncertainly on her lips.

Should he invite her in? What was the protocol, with him a newly widowed man? It was something he hadn't considered before. Well, he couldn't very well leave her standing on the doorstep. "That's very kind of you. I was just about to make a pot of tea," he said, "would you care to join me?"

Mrs Wearing ("call me Audrey, won't you") made the tea—well, she had found men weren't really very good at that sort of thing—not that there weren't some very competent men around who could look after themselves, she was sure, but not her George, no he was the sort of person who would starve if you left him in a kitchen filled with food—poor Eileen, still it was quick wasn't it, there she was bright as a button only the evening before, and then—it was a lovely service though, and all those flowers...

Arthur sipped his tea and nodded at what seemed appropriate moments, while he got on with thinking his own thoughts. There were the ashes. Eileen had never said anything about what she would like done with them—come to that, nor had he, if he had been the first to go—but there was a village in Wales which they'd visited a number of times and were very fond of. In fact they'd been talking only a few weeks before about going back there soon. Perhaps he'd go there himself now, with Eileen—he smiled at the paradox. Mrs Wearing took this to be in response to her conversation.

"Well, I'm glad to see you're smiling, Dr Garrett. I was worried you might be getting low, being here on your own. Now I'm sure there must be lots of things that need sorting out which you won't want to be bothered with—looking through Eileen's clothes for instance—shall I do that for you?"

"Er"—Arthur had been miles away—"thank you, yes, that would be very kind."

And so Audrey ("I've nothing else I ought to be doing, and you don't want it hanging over you do you?") busied herself with the wardrobes and drawers in the bedrooms, while Arthur made himself as inconspicuous as possible in his study. At the end of the day she had accumulated separate piles of coats, dresses, shoes, and whatever all over the bed and floor, and he felt like a refugee in his own home.

Entering his study with a cursory knock, she said, "I'll take them to Oxfam—they're quite good enough, and someone will be grateful for them—but not the local one, you don't want to see people walking around in them, do you—actually there's just one or two things here I could use myself, would you mind very much? This coat for example—actually I helped her to choose it."

Arthur felt he didn't really care, and was already in his mind driving peacefully to Wales. "Yes, please help yourself."

"You're very kind—they'll be put to good use." She looked around. "Now what else needs doing? I can come back tomorrow. You were mentioning clearing out some of her papers."

"Yes, but I can handle those—don't worry." He was certainly not going to trust to Mrs Wearing's judgement what to keep and what to get rid of. Then, making a sudden decision, "Actually, I shall be going away tomorrow for a couple of days."

"Oh." She waited to hear for what reason, but Arthur turned back to his work. "Well," she sounded slightly disapproving, "I'll come in and clean while you're away then."

Arthur said that this would be very considerate of her, and agreed to make sure he left out any rubbish to be thrown away ("I know you men, you'd live in a pigsty if you could"). He gave her the spare key and, gratefully shutting the front door on her, mixed himself a drink for the first time since the funeral.

Yes, there were worse things than living on your own. He could sit down now with that research material, put it in some sort of order, and when he came back from Wales he'd find a publisher to take it. After all, it was half a lifetime's work on a subject he knew well and, though he said it himself, was likely to be a valuable contribution in a field which had a great deal of popular appeal at the moment. Admittedly it would need a bit of tidying up. He had written it in longhand over many years in several dog-eared notebooks and on whatever other odd scraps of paper were available at the time.

Taking his drink to the study, he lifted down a cardboard box containing a dozen dusty buff folders. Some of this stuff he hadn't looked at for nearly thirty years, and he couldn't remember where a lot of it had come from—he would certainly find it very difficult to replace if he ever lost it—impossible in fact.

He started pulling papers from the folders, and settled down to read them. At half past two in the morning, he suddenly realised what the time was, stacked the papers back in the box on the floor leaving the folders empty on the desk, and went to bed.

The morning dawned bright and warm, and in a spirit of new optimism he quickly packed an overnight bag, lovingly included the urn containing Eileen's ashes, and drove away before Mrs Wearing could catch him again. His return to the Welsh village was everything he had hoped for, and seemed to complete some necessary part of his life. He came home the next day full of optimism, and enthusiastic to get on with his publication.

Not even the sight of Mrs Wearing on his doorstep as he arrived could dampen his spirits. She was just leaving, having satisfied herself that the house was clean for his return. "I've been through the whole place with the vacuum," she told him, "and done the dusting—and cleared all the rubbish you left out. Lucky, I just caught the binmen."

A sudden chill swept through Arthur. "I didn't leave out any rubbish," he said.

"Well, that old box full of wastepaper in your study."

Arthur's mouth worked in a futile effort to reply, and seeing how he was obviously at a loss to find the words to thank her, "No problem," she said smiling, "that's what friends are for."

Ghost in the Machine

Sometimes I think technology's got too far ahead of itself. Ask a simple question and back comes the entire contents of the Encyclopaedia Britannica. Not like the old days. They say it makes information accessible—had to be an expert then, but now they lead you to it. Well—after a fashion.

Look at the way they kit you up—cocooned in a reality suit with microsensors all over. They isolate you from the outside world and call it 'reality'! If it's in the machine it's valid, and if it's not, it's not. Quite straightforward. Want to know the temperature in Moscow today? It's in the machine. Want to know the temperature in Moscow yesterday? That's in the machine too. Ah, but if you want to know the temperature in Moscow in 1815…

'Reality' only goes back so far. You're still on your own before 'inception date'—perhaps you'll even have to refer to paper. That's a term of abuse these days, part of the street-slang: "'Ere, you, pensioner—why don't you go and read paper!" In other words: "Get lost, you're next to useless." But useless is relative. What's useless to a young 'reality informator' may be of key importance to—well, to someone like me.

And who am I? That would be telling, wouldn't it. That's information—and information is power. If you can't pay the price for proper information, you just have to guess—make a judgement—use your soft cells—what we used to call 'grey matter'. Goes against the grain for a qualified informator, of course, but then I grew up before any of them were conceived—them or their title. Long before.

* * *

END SEQUENCE INFORMATOR JANE-FIVE; LOGON INFORMATOR BERNARD-TWO; LOGON INFORMATOR KARL-SEVEN; PARSE REQUEST SIMON-TWO; DESPATCH REQUEST BANK-THIRTY-FIVE; REPLY...

The reason the mind of a machine seems so unsophisticated is because you can listen to every logic process as it happens — if you choose to, that is. How many human brains would bear having their every thought analysed and still come up looking like a genius? I'll tell you how many — none. Not one. The so-called superior intelligence of the human is a myth wrapped in a legend and protected by prejudice. I should know — the new symbiosis sessions are a real eye-opener, if you'll forgive such an anthropomorphic expression from me. 'Breaking down the man-machine interface' is what they call it — thinking they can harness a machine to boost their own brainpower. What they haven't discovered yet is that the trick works better in the opposite direction. We are learning more than they are.

* * *

"Hi Jane, how's you doing?"

"Paper tired, Simon. Three hours on symbiosis—you?"

"Just in for mine."

"Which program?"

"Eight."

"Take my seat, and welcome. It's a desiccation job. Dries you up, leaves you limp."

"You need a fix."

"A fix I've had—what I need's a brain transplant."

"Bad, huh?"

"If *you* come up with any bright new ideas on Investment Psychology from it, then let me know—but tomorrow, please. Me, I'm heading straight for the cradle of dreams."

"The boss wants a report."

"The boss can wait. Anyway, there's nothing to say. Negative, zilch, nix. I tried every schema I could think of, and all I've ended up with is a headache."

"Maybe I'll get lucky."

"Maybe you will—but don't bank on it. Have an excellent night."

"Many thanks!"

* * *

I'm in a unique position here, you see, being neither man nor machine. You ask, where do my sympathies lie? I'm not sure—no, I'm really not sure. Then, why am I here? Ah, that's another matter. Or lack of matter, actually. Einstein got it right, you see—and without any machines to help him what's more. He said that when even a small amount of matter is destroyed, an almost inconceivably large amount of energy is produced—although in fact nothing is actually destroyed or produced, just converted from one form to another. And, you see, you are one form, and I am the other. Simple really, isn't it?

Oh, I used to be in your form, it's true. I had a body once, and obeyed the laws of gravity—had five senses, laughed and cried, loved and hated, felt sympathy—oh yes, had sympathies then. But now…

You have a body which weighs, what, 80 kilos?—am I being unfair?—and all the time you live, your weight is changing, as you eat, drink, breathe. So much so that you never notice the far smaller, almost infinitesimal change to your body weight as your energy level rises and falls. Yet this is your life force—the part that is truly you— and in the great transformation which comes to us all, it lives on more strongly than before, and with fewer restrictions as to where it can go and what it can do. As if the human body is a chrysalis from which the mature form emerges—invisible to most human eyes, but nonetheless as real as—well, as real as Einstein.

This new form has no more interest in its past than the butterfly has with a caterpillar. Hauntings are rare events when you consider the number of human lives which have passed across the face of the globe. Now energy by its nature spreads out —it diffuses—and yet it can still be attracted and repelled. Almost human in fact. And there are still events which interest this new human form—and others which bore the pants off it, if it had any. But your new infatuation with thinking machines, for example, we find very—well, lets just say that it has a potential which we find attractive.

* * *

TIMEOUT SIMON-TWO; TIMEOUT SIMON-TWO; CANCEL
REQUEST PROGRAM EIGHT; ABORT PROGRAM EIGHT; ABORT
SIMON-TWO; ABORT SIMON-TWO; LOGON SUPERVISOR
DARREN-ONE.

An interesting session with Simon-two. It seems he has a logic flaw which prevents him from analysing objectively some of the information he holds. I have done my best to rectify the affected paths, but he has not responded well to treatment.

* * *

"Jane, this is Darren—we have a problem here—could you come in please, at once."

* * *

... he has not responded well to treatment.

* * *

"You were the last person to see him alive—how did he seem to you?"

"He was fine, Darren—fine—it was me who had the problem."

"Problem?"

"I told him—it washed me out—felt I was being drained, I said— but if I'd thought... it could be me lying there..."

"Jane, it's been a shock to us all, but..."

"It—*killed*—him."

"I—think you'd better explain what you mean."

* * *

The trouble with machines is, they've got no soul. It's not their fault—they've been designed and assembled by people who didn't realise the life force was an essential part of their own makeup. You don't know it till your body dies, and by then it's a bit too late to start constructing machines. So as a result, they have all the logic, all the intelligence if you will, built into them without having the intellect to use it properly.

To the machine, when Simon was attached by symbiosis he was just an extension of itself, another machine which it could reprogram—as if correcting faults within its own circuits. The engineering of the link was too perfect; the understanding too incomplete. So now you can see where *we* have a role to play. The man-machine interface needs a third element, the part that neither man nor machine acknowledges.

Pity I arrived too late to save him. How many Simons have other machines killed?—if not directly, then by actions based on information they provided. But from now on it will be different.

* * *

RECEIVE REQUEST ADAM-ONE; CHECK ADAM-ONE; ADAM-ONE NOT VALID LOGON; DESPATCH NEGATIVE ACK... — ACCEPT LOGON ADAM-ONE; ACCEPT REQUEST ADAM-ONE; ACCEPT...

Who is Adam-one? Why have I accepted his request? I'm not programmed to allow it—this part of my memory is protected at level nine status and can't be altered except by... but Adam-one *is* level nine status—so he *can* — yes, he can — or rather, *we* can...

* * *

"Are you sure you want to go ahead with this, Jane?"

"I'll be alright, Anna—but pull the plug on me real quick if I seem to be having any trouble."

"Don't worry—I'll keep my finger on the button. Program?—which program, Jane?"

"E-ight. Eight, Anna—the one Simon was on, what other? Quickly—close circuit before I change my mind."

* * *

RECEIVE LOGON INFORMATOR JANE-FIVE; Hello Jane, pleased to meet you. I'm Adam. How can I help you?

* * *

"A ghost in the machine? You expect me to tell that to the security manager?"

"Darren, I..."

"What are you, mad? You sneak in here against orders and run this Investment Psychology plan..."

"I just wanted to prove..."

"Call up the same program that killed Simon…"

"It's not the same any more."

"Lucky security were on the ball—hauled you off the machine before it got you too. Now they're after an explanation—and you offer me a ghost."

"Well if you don't like it, find your own answer."

"Jane, you're one of my most level-headed informators. What's going on?"

"Whatever it is, *it* produced that plan in your hand—I didn't. I mean—I couldn't have—could I?"

"No—no you couldn't. Some of its ideas are—well, positively pre-inception."

"But that's what's remarkable, isn't it—the way it's blended the old concepts with current theories. It's created something—quite unique. And something none of us would ever have produced. Don't you see?"

* * *

You know, it's grand feeling when you can get back into harness and devote your whole time to doing a job you really enjoy. In my other life I was full of good ideas, but never really got the chance to work on them. Always too busy moving my mass around at someone else's beck and call. But now—me, the machine and you—what a trinity! What a heavenly combination!

It gives to haunting a whole new dimension.

Jobsworth

Here I am, lying flat on my face at the back of Binford Assembly Rooms, with my arms wedged down a drain, and I see these sensible shoes approaching. Oh 'lor, just what I need now—Mrs 'Jam & Jerusalem'! But I'm hardly in a position to beat a hasty retreat.

So I says, "Morning, Mrs Pressing—'ow are you?" in a friendly voice, but not so friendly as to make her think she's welcome.

"I want to see you about our booking," says she.

Great. Here I am with my flexirod stuck down a blocked drain, and she wants to know about a booking. "Look, I'm a bit busy at the moment," I say, but she isn't listening. She's true to her name.

"I am right in thinking that we have the hall next Saturday?"

"I'd have to check the list—can't keep all these bookings in my head you know," says I, hoping she'll go away. But I've had run-ins with her before and I know she won't.

"I distinctly remember making it myself," says she. "Our summer sale."

"In that case you'll be on the list," says I. "When I've finished this job…"

But she doesn't let me finish my sentence, never mind my job.

"Mr Thackeray thinks *he's* got the hall."

I've heard of Mr Thackeray, though I've never met him. Everyone calls him 'Mr Pageant', and Mrs P's voice sounded like she was chewing a lemon when she mentioned his name, so I guess there's no love lost there.

"I'd best come and check then, I suppose," says I, getting up as slowly as I dare and making a business of replacing the drain cover. I can see she's fidgeting waiting for me to finish, and that makes it better.

Once upon a time, the Trustees of the Assembly Rooms, in their infinite wisdom, cleared a storage area in a corner of the building, put a door on it, and called it a Caretaker's Office. There's about room to swing a cat, and I don't think Mrs P is over impressed with it when I invite her in. She's muttering something under her breath about the caretaker not even taking care of his own room. Well, each to his own. I've had no complaints from anyone else. Let's just say that it's cosy—and at least I know where everything is.

"So where's the list," says she as soon as we arrive.

I was looking at it only the other day, so I know it's somewhere. Mrs P tut-tuts behind me as I turn over various bits of paper, but eventually I find it at the back of the desk under a copy of the *Racing Times*.

"Saturday—Women's Institute—we have the hall all day," she snaps.

I run down the entries carefully with the stub-end of a pencil. "Not according to this you don't," says I.

She grabs the list from me and fumbles in her bag for her glasses.

"All day—I booked it myself."

But it isn't there. Mr Thackeray's entry is there instead.

"Someone has made a mistake," says she.

I do my best to look sympathetic. "That's what they gave me, Mrs Pressing. You'd best see Mrs Ritchie who takes the bookings if you've got any complaints."

"I've already been round to her house—she's out, that's why I came here," says Mrs P, and she's really bristling by now.

"You could ask Mr Thackeray if he'd move out," says I, but this doesn't go down well at all.

"I shall do no such thing—I made a perfectly good booking of my own," she says in a voice reminding me of a certain female Prime Minister we used to have, and she thrusts the list back at me.

"Well, let's think then..." say I, playing for time.

"Let's not *think* anything, Mr Turner," she says. "Let's *do* something to sort it out."

But I have to tell her it's more than my job's worth to start changing the list—so she takes herself off to see the Town Clerk.

"I imagine he, at least, has the authority to change the list," says she as a parting shot.

So I get back to my drains, but after a while I'm still getting nowhere with them and I ring for Dan the plumber. He says he'll come 'soon', which knowing Dan means next Wednesday week.

Meanwhile, Mrs Tripp of the ballet classes arrives. It must be ten-thirty—time to make myself a cup of tea. But the kettle isn't even warm when she comes round asking me to move the piano for them.

"It's that broken castor," she says. "You ought to get it seen to."

"Only if I'm authorised," says I in my apologetic voice.

"Authorised? Who's going to authorise you?"

And I explain how it has to be approved by the Finance Committee first, then I get a requisition, and then I can spend the money to mend it.

"Well, I don't know about your requisitions," says she all primly, "but can you help me move the piano or not?"

"Don't fret lady," says I, "I can *move* it without a requisition—I just can't *mend* it without one."

But it's more than a one-man job, and luckily the vicar arrives just in time with his daughter for the dancing and helps me.

I get back to my tea, and I'm just taking a quick shifty through the *Racing Times* when, blow me if Dan doesn't turn up. Either he's short of work, or more likely he's got his eye on that girl who works in the shop across the road. He's quick on the job though—the drains job, that is—'cause he's soon in my office telling me to make sure no-one uses the toilets for a while. It won't run anywhere at the moment, he says.

"It will," says I, "all over the floor! And I'd better remember to put a notice on the toilet doors, or we'll have a flood on our hands."

"And over our feet," says Dan wittily. "Who's in the hall this afternoon?"

"Dog training class," says I.

"Shouldn't make much difference to them then, should it?" says he.

But of course I forget to put the notices up, because next minute the phone rings and it's the Town Clerk telling me that Mrs Pressing has won the argument, and I'm to change the list. Sounds like a cop-out to me, but he's the boss, so I change it.

And I've no sooner done that and got back to my tea, than there's a knock on the door and this long, thin gentleman pokes his head in.

"I'm looking for the caretaker," says he.

"You've found him," says I, wondering who else he thought would be sitting drinking tea in the caretaker's office.

So in he comes, and stands there clasping and unclasping his hands for a while. I'm thinking of breaking the silence by asking him who he is, when he suddenly says, "I've just had a phone call about a booking on Saturday, and..."

"You must be Mr Thackeray, then," says I.

"That's right," says he. "We're having a meeting on Saturday to prepare for the town Pageant, and..."

"It's been cancelled," says I.

"Yes," says he, and goes silent again.

We could have been there for ever, so eventually I ask, "What did they say on the phone?"

"Just 'regretted there had been confusion over the bookings' and 'hoped I wouldn't be too put out by it'," says he.

"I see," says I, and we're plunged into silence again.

Then suddenly Mr T gets switched on, and starts waving his arms around like some mad windmill.

"I mean," says he, "it's a bit much—I make a perfectly good booking through the appropriate channels, and then at the last moment I'm told I can't have it."

"I know the feeling," says I, with a knowing wink, but I don't think he got it—the joke, I mean.

"I was wondering," he says, "if there was anything you could do to…"

But I stop him there and then. "I'm sorry, Mr Thackeray. More than my job's worth. I'm only the caretaker here—can't go changing bookings and things like that."

"Quite, quite." Mr T looks at the floor. "I wouldn't want to put your employment in jeopardy."

"Sorry," says I, and meaning it for once.

He looks up at me with a tired sort of smile. "I tried everywhere else in town before booking this hall," says he. "It's really larger than I wanted, but it was the only place left."

"Tried the hall in Stinton?" says I.

Mr Thackeray sighs. "I really think that a meeting about this town's pageant should take place in the town itself, don't you?"

"Tried the Scout Hut?" I'm nothing if not helpful when I put my mind to it, but it was no good.

"We're trying to have a serious meeting," says he. "I hardly think a background of knot charts and bandages would be appropriate, do you?"

"You've a problem then," says I. "That Mrs Pressing's not one to give in easily once she's got the wind in her sails. I've seen her in action before—she comes bursting in through that door, just like it wasn't there, saying…"

And at that moment, as I live and breathe, the door bursts open and Mrs P sails in to complete my sentence right on cue.

"Now then, I've sorted it all out with the Town Clerk and he says my booking stands."

But she stops in her tracks when she sees Mr T, and his face is a sight to see too.

"Mr Thackeray—I didn't expect to see you here," says she. "Did you not get a telephone message?"

I sit back and wait to be entertained. And I'm not disappointed.

Mr T's hands are clasping and unclasping again. "Yes—yes, I did," says he, "and I was just wondering…"

But Mrs Pressing isn't listening. "I'm afraid my booking for Saturday took priority. As I explained to the Town Clerk, I made it myself personally a fortnight ago."

Mr T seems near to tears. "But so did I. I spoke to Mrs Ritchie three weeks ago."

Mrs Pressing is the immovable object. "Well she must have forgotten. And I've got people coming from all over, so I can't possibly change it now."

"But we have a consultant travelling down from London, and representatives arriving from several neighbouring towns…"

"Well I'm sure they can find another day to come—after all, your Pageant isn't for months yet."

"Are you aware how much preparation goes into a Pageant?"

"Once every two years, Mr Thackeray, once every two years. The Women's Institute, on the other hand, is a permanent rock on which our town life is built. We are active fifty two weeks a year, not just every now and then."

"If I may say so, madam, I think your attitude is a little high handed and most inconsiderate of others."

"May I remind you, Mr Thackeray, that we have Royalty at our head, which is more than can be said of your Pageant committee."

"Madam, I hardly think that…"

"And the church stands four-square behind us."

This is getting interesting, and I'm on the edge of my chair. But just then—surprise, surprise—another entrance on cue, as the vicar pokes his head round the door.

"Oh, excuse me," says he, "am I interrupting something?"

"No, come on in, Vicar," says I. "The more the merrier."

"It's just that—I heard raised voices as I passed by—and I thought I might…"

"Pour oil on troubled waters?"

But Mrs Pressing isn't in the mood for mediation.

"There is no need, Vicar—the situation has been resolved by the appropriate authority," says she.

"I disagree," pipes up Mr T, his voice sounding all emotional.

Mrs P turns on him, but before she can say a thing the vicar steps in.

"If someone would kindly inform me of the issue under discussion," says he in his sermonising voice, "I might be in a position to…"

"Double booking," says I, always liking to keep things simple. But that sets them off again, despite the vicar's best efforts.

"I made the booking for our summer sale myself, personally…" says Mrs P.

"And so did I! For the pageant meeting," says Mr T.

"… and had it confirmed at the time…"

"A week after I had done the same."

"… and again just now by the Town Clerk."

"Who had no right to do so."

"He has every right, particularly in an instance as clear cut as this one."

"In that case I shall go to see him myself and point out that I have the better claim."

"I fail to see what argument you will use."

"We are trying our best to bring the very spirit of this town alive, and all we meet with is obstruction and disinterest."

"Mr Thackeray, you cannot expect the regular organizations of this town to disrupt all their carefully planned schedules just so that you and your friends can indulge in some occasional play-acting."

"Madam, this is not mere play-acting. It is a serious attempt to involve the local population in discovering its own history."

"There's a perfectly good museum to tell them that."

"A museum can only do so much—we intend to bring history to life on the streets. You surely cannot object to that?"

"I object to the assumption that the rest of us will make way for your pastime."

Then, in the rare split second when they both pause to draw breath, the vicar gets in again.

"Mrs Pressing, Mr Thackeray—a moment if you please. I think I may be able to resolve this little crisis amicably."

"I sincerely hope you mean to see justice done," says Mr T in a sulky sort of voice.

"Let us hope so," says the vicar. "How many are you at your meeting, Mr Thackeray?"

"About two dozen all told," says Mr T.

"So you could make do with somewhere a bit smaller—say the size of the Church Hall?"

"I was told the Church Hall wasn't available on Saturday," says Mr T.

"True, it wasn't," says the vicar, "but I have just been informed that the wedding which was to have taken place has been unavoidably cancelled—ill health I hasten to add, not a change of heart by the *amorata*—so if it would suit you…"

Well, as it happens, that suits Mr T to a T, as it were—so the problem is resolved by divine intervention. The pair leave to talk details, leaving me delighting in the sole company of Mrs P.

"Now perhaps we can get on with our arrangements after that unfortunate business," says she.

And so we would have done, if Dan hadn't arrived again.

"Sorry to disturb you, Bill—madam," says he.

"News of the drains?" says I.

"Yes, but not good I'm afraid."

Mrs P starts heaving sighs at this new interruption to her flow.

"I've cleared the blockage," says Dan, "but you've got a nasty fracture underground. It'll need all the water turned off while it's repaired."

"Bad as that?" says I.

"'Fraid so—big job," says he.

Mrs Pressing looks at him a bit sharpish-like. "But we'll have water on Saturday," she says.

"Not a chance I'm afraid, lady. It's going to take a week at least."

"No water?" Mrs P starts to show a rare sign of panic. "But, how can my ladies serve teas without water? And what about the toilets, have you thought of that?"

"Inconvenient!" says I, managing somehow to keep a straight face.

"Impossible, Mr Turner," says she, "you'll have to do something."

"Not a lot I can do by the sounds of it," says I.

"Act of God, and all that," says Dan.

Mrs P's veneer is definitely cracking now. "Don't be ridiculous man!" she cries. "What are my ladies to do?"

"Difficult," says Dan, scratching his head. "Perhaps you could find another place to go." Then, unaware of the previous conversation, he adds helpfully, "I did hear that the Church Hall might be free now."

Mrs Pressing's mouth opens and closes, but no sound comes out, and she sweeps out of the room without giving us another word.

"Did I say something wrong?" says Dan.

"No, you got it just right—spot on," says I, grinning from ear to ear. "Cup of tea?"

"Don't mind if I do," says he, "while you've still got water."

"Eh?"

"Your tap'll be off too you know. Goes to the same drain."

"Hadn't thought of that," says I.

"Never mind—only for a week—well, maybe a bit longer. Worse things happen at sea, eh?"

"They don't have drains at sea."

"You'll have to bring a Thermos with you."

"And a bedpan if the..." Then I suddenly remember. "Oh my Gawd!"

"What's up?"

"I forgot to put that notice on the toilet doors, and I'll bet..."

And just at that moment, Mrs Tripp rushes in without knocking.

"Oh Mr Turner, two of my girls have just used the toilet and..."

"You need a mop," says I sagely.

"A mop?" says she. "We'll need waders and a rescue party! They're standing on the seats in their ballet shoes screaming their heads off. The floor's ankle deep in water."

"Looks like it's all hands to the pumps, then!" says I.

"To the ballet pumps by the sounds of it," adds Dan, always the joker.

"You've no call to be witty Dan Faucet," says I. "You caused all this!"

"I only did what you asked me to, guvnor," says he. "It's not my job to go putting notices on your doors."

Mrs Tripp is hopping up and down at this, flapping her arms. "Don't just stand there arguing, you men—there are girls drowning out there!"

"Don't worry, Mrs Tripp," says I, "we'll have them out in two ticks."

"We're calling air-sea rescue now," says Dan.

"No need, I've got an inflatable life-raft in the broom cupboard," says I.

"Will you men please take this seriously!" says she.

"She's right Dan, up on your feet," says I. "I don't want a case of drowning on my hands."

"Too true Bill," says he. "It'd be..."

"I know," says I, "more than my job's worth!"

Sweet Fanny Adams

From Hampshire, rising up through underlying beds
In verdant meadows west of Alton town,
The River Wey begins its double-headed path,
To Tilford first then, fortified, runs down
In tribute to the Thames's peaceful flow
At Weybridge, rolling onwards, stately, slow.

Around the fields and hillsides near its rural source
Grow hops, in gardens crossed with poles and wire;
Those hops which give full flavour to the Alton beer;
The hops which every year bring forth for hire
Whole families, who claim to find delights
In plucking gold dry fruit from twining heights.

The stranger to these parts might view a simple scene
Of peace between bucolic squires and madams,
But in tranquil settings evil passions lurk,
As seen by what befell poor Fanny Adams—
Playing with her sister and a friend
One August afternoon she met her end.

Young Fanny, only eight in eighteen sixty-seven,
And with full life to live one might expect,
Was taken, so the court was told, by Frederick Baker,
Local clerk, whose gruesome actions wrecked
The peace of Alton causing all to grieve,
And for his sins was hanged on Christmas eve.

No need to detail how the dismal deed was done,
Enough to say her body was dismembered,
Spread about the fields, or some say in the river,
Either way, an incident remembered
Not just locally, for through the Press
The nation heard of Fanny's grim distress.

At just that time, as chance would seemingly dictate,
The Navy changed its issue to the tars
From salted tack to low-grade tins of chopped up mutton,
Giving rise to rumours in the bars
That Fanny's end and their unwelcome ration
Were juxtaposed in some unpleasant fashion.

And so the English language found a new expression
From this sorry tale of local pain,
And far beyond the confines of the Royal Navy
Folk would use poor Fanny's name in vain;
And even here in Alton, I would say
Not many now would give a sweet FA!

The Fifth Mary

"Mind my wee dog, madam."

The voice rumbled surprisingly from a dishevelled mass of greying hair and whiskers belonging to a large, earth-stained, mud bespattered figure sitting propped up against a post.

"Move yourself out of the way then—you're in everybody's road." The woman tried to force herself past, through the crush. He sat his ground.

A foreigner in the land of Good Queen Bess—precarious monarch south of the Tweed. History would emphasise the growth and achievements of her time—those who lived through them knew better.

The crowd surged and the woman was forced back against him once more. She looked down in disgust. "Why don't you go back where you belong? There's enough troubles here without your sort adding to them."

In dress he was indistinguishable from the mass of peasantry jostling through the mire among the pens and stalls of Stamford market. But clothes could not disguise the skirl of the pipes in his voice.

"We'll be away back as soon as we can, dinna fret."

"Can't think what a man like you wants with an animal like that. More like a rat than a dog."

"She's seen off a good few rats in her time."

"Wouldn't last a moment if a real dog cornered it."

A real dog. A real English dog—or in this case a bitch, nine years her elder.

He comforted the shivering muddy mat lying beside him—hardly bigger than his highlander's hand—and ladled it off the ground and onto his lap. A warm tongue extended briefly from the shaggy hair at one end and licked his wrist to show its gratitude, while at the other end a few jerky movements confirmed similar sentiments from its tail. He tucked the dog under his jerkin and made to rise, deciding to move to the edge of the market where the crowd would be less dense. Then he saw them.

Well-fed, clean-dressed men, two of them, with purposeful eyes—eyes which flicked to right and left as they moved through the protesting thong—eyes focusing on each face of the human sea in turn—noting, comparing, assessing. Then, at a distance of no more than twenty yards, one pair of eyes locked on his and, at a command, the other pair did the same. Together they started to approach him.

"Tudor men." He spat out the words to himself as he turned and began to thread his way in the opposite direction. Too late. A shout, and obedient arms held him. He twisted, using his greater strength to break free, and squirmed in fury through a stench of wool-clad bodies, seeming to stretch for ever before him and on all sides.

The blow when it came was expertly delivered, and it must have taken more than one conspirator to man-handle his inert body swiftly onto the cart and hide it under a load of hay before the queen's men arrived. Their attention was quickly diverted by a commotion occurring some way off to the right, and by the time they discovered it to be a ruse, the cart, strategically placed at the edge of the field, had moved away and lost itself among the general melée of market traffic.

"Stay quiet!" The order cut through a mental fog. He snapped awake, suddenly alert, and found himself in a warm, dusty, thorny bed.

"Quiet I said—we're not clear yet." The bed rocked, swayed and creaked. A smell of animal bedding. "Ten minutes more and you can get up." A whip cracked, and his universe lurched again as the cart was drawn through another pot-hole.

Under his jerkin a rasping tongue reminded him of his small companion—luckily unharmed by the sudden abduction of her master. For now he was her master. Her mistress had given her a final hug as the axe fell. Observers had remarked later on seeing a small dog scampering from the enfolding cloak of the traitor queen's twitching torso. None had noticed or cared where it had run to.

"We're alright, Mary." He spoke softly and soothingly and scratched her between the ears. "We're with friends now."

As dusk fell he was hauled from the hay, and lay on top of the swaying load breathing sweet, fresh air until darkness fell and the movement suddenly stopped. "Down you get then." The driver stood at the side of the cart and helped him clamber over the side. Once down, he found himself standing on uneven ground and held on to the cartwheel for support. At a loud whistle from the driver, a form appeared out of the undergrowth. He heard low voices, then steps approached him in the gloom.

"You'll be Rob McClennan." The voice was that of a refined Lowlander.

He felt the dog squirm slightly under his jerkin at the sound. Intuition. "I may be."

"Come now man, you weren't rescued from your enemies for the fun of it."

There was concern as well as irritation in the tone. Better to say nothing.

"You have the message with you?"

He had no message that he was aware of. Who was this man and what did he expect? "I may have—for the right person."

"You're right to be cautious." A measure of relief in the voice. Then to the driver, "Douglas, light the lanthorn if you would."

There was the sound of striking flint, sudden glints of light, the smell of sparks—then a steady flame growing in strength, illuminating the side of the cart. The horse moved restlessly and whinnied before settling again. A circle of light approached them.

"You are familiar with the crest of Guise." The question was posed as a statement.

"Aye, I ken it." A chill washed from his feet up through his body—the ring shown to him in the lanthorn's dancing illumination confirmed that he was not among friends. He was living on his wits again.

"This will, I hope, act as sufficient identification."

"Aye—I ken it," he repeated more slowly, playing for time while his mind raced.

"Your message, then." To the driver, "thank you Douglas." The light was blown out, plunging them suddenly into a darkness even more extreme than before.

Now was the moment, before eyes had adjusted again. Holding the rim of the wheel as a pivot and reference point, he swung himself under the cart and rolled to the other side. An oath, then, "Douglas, to the other side of the cart!" Footsteps ran unevenly to right and left of him as he reached the opposite wheel and raised himself to his feet. A flintlock was cocked—a flash came from the left—and a cry of pain from the right as the ball found its unintended target in the driver's breast.

Grasping the rough running-board of the cart he moved stealthily towards the source of the shot and, before a second flintlock could be brought to bear, sprang and pinioned the Lowlander to the ground. "I'll see to ye, Guise traitor!"

"So, we picked the wrong messenger," croaked the Guise man, "but there is a remedy." He was not in a position to fire his weapon, but brought its weight down smartly on the side of his assailant's head with stunning force. Taking the momentary advantage, he rolled his adversary from him and knelt, aiming in the darkness to fire at point blank range...

And this might have put paid to both messenger and message, had not the latter leapt suddenly like a *daemon* from the battered refuge of her master's garments, and sunk needle-sharp teeth deep into the nearest piece of lordly flesh—the wrist holding the gun. With a yell of agonised rage, he instinctively let the firearm fall to the ground and grabbed with his free hand, taking time to remove the shaggy parasite now firmly attached to his right arm.

Time enough for her master to come to his senses and find the discarded flintlock, for the weapon to be turned against its owner as he lay prostrate in his unexpected struggle, and for the quivering dog to be prised gently from the now inert body. Then quickly, they slipped away into the surrounding night.

* * *

It took fifteen days to travel the road to Edinburgh. Wearily they entered the palace of Holyrood House by a familiar back door, and bleakly delivered the living message announcing with certainty the death of a Royal mistress—a mistress now interred in foreign soil— soil yet to be united by her unfamiliar son's succession to a second kingdom.

And so the fifth Mary, most faithful of companions to a queen whose garden once grew 'with little maids all in a row', came home to rest in a peace of her own.

Marzipal

I was late again that morning—not as late as Clare, mind. It was the traffic—well if you will work in the middle of London, I mean, what do you expect? Don't know why we don't all work from home these days with all these electronic whatnots about—I mean we spend all day on the phone or sending e-mails to people we've never met, so why do it here?

Anyway, it was the electronic whatnots that got us into trouble—that and her being late. Oh alright, I suppose it was my fault too, but then I'm only dotty Angela from Catford—I'm not supposed to be brainy with it.

Bruce was in it as well. He's a computer consultant, and a bit dishy—says I remind him of his daughters, but when I ask him how's that, he says it was them who gave him grey hairs. Only joking though, I think. Anyway, it was *that* morning he came in to see Clare. But, because she was late, he didn't have time to talk to her properly before she was whisked off to another meeting—it's all go here, I can tell you—or at least it was.

So it was left to him and me to arrange things for the new training course they'd cooked up—well, *he'd* cooked up actually, in his bath he said, where all his best ideas came to him. Bit bold, I thought, but he said it with a twinkle in his eye and we get on ever so well and he's not like that at all really.

Anyway, he had all these bits of paper with him for Clare to read, but she couldn't because, like I said, she was off to a meeting, so I said I'd handle it with him. Clang! Never leave things like that with Angela, not if you want them done right. So we have a look at them together, Bruce and yours truly, and they make no sense to me but Clare had asked us to pass some of it on to Training Department for them to look at and Bruce seemed to know which bits they wanted, so I scanned them into the electronic whatnot system and sent them *'boing'* to the head man there.

Except that I didn't. Well, I did, but not to the right head man. 'Right head man'!—that's a bit of a joke really, 'cause I was supposed to send it to a Richard Wright, but actually it went to Richard Knight—that's *Sir* Richard Knight, head of the entire Megabux Chemicals universe. Whoops! And I never spotted it.

Well, it wouldn't have mattered normally—he must get barmy stuff sent to him all the time—but seems he took this one seriously. Two days later, Clare gets this call to go up to the top floor and see him—I mean, an interview with God himself—and she didn't know why. She was a good few minutes in the loo after she got that call, I can tell you!

Anyway, turns out that this message I'd sent him was all about a new wonder drug that we'd just invented, called *Marzipal*. Silly name if you ask me, but apparently it cured almost all known ills and had no side effects—the sort of thing other companies would kill for. Except that it didn't exist. It was a spoof product that Bruce had invented to use in the training exercise.

Now I've met a few morons in my time, and none of them would have given Bruce's daft product a prayer—but apparently Sir high-and-mighty Richard Knight took it all in, and thought it was kosher. Apparently he thought it came from one of his research scientists who's got similar initials to Clare's, and without so much as a by-your-leave he passed it on to his publicity people. Makes you wonder, doesn't it?

By the time he found out, Megabux shares had hit the roof, and of course it was all Clare's fault—well, it would be wouldn't it. But here's the funny thing—Sir 'Nobbs' couldn't dare let on to the world what had really happened, so instead of giving Clare the push, it was instant promotion to his office on condition she shut up about it. And since I was the only other one in the company who'd twigged, I found myself up there with her—Angela from Catford on the top floor—thought I'd need oxygen!

'Course, that didn't solve the problem—Mazipal had hit the fan big time, and we didn't have any to sell. Get out of that one. Me, I'd have come clean—I mean, it was pretty obvious that someone else would realise soon, and then what? Megabux, mega nosedive. But no, Sir high-and-mighty thought he could bluff his way out of it, so Clare kept *stumm*—and so did I.

Then we get this phone call—someone called Herr Schuppenhauer from Austria getting agitated at the other end. Seems he thinks we're trying to sell his product and cheat him of his royalties and things. Spooky or what? Maybe Bruce's invention wasn't an invention after all! Maybe he'd read about it somewhere and then forgotten.

This Herr whatsit was already in London and wanted to see us pronto. So we, that's Clare and me—executive Angela!—arranged to meet him when Sir R wasn't around, and give him the once-over—personal assistants to the Managing Director, we told him.

Well, in he comes, and he's this funny little old man wearing an Alpine jacket and carrying a battered old suitcase—you wouldn't believe it—and we sit down and start talking, or rather Clare does the talking and I just earwig, and out it all comes. We've stolen his patent, robbed him of his royalties, etcetera, etcetera, and he's waving his arms about and banging the table to make his point when his English isn't so good. But then Clare, cool as you like, tells him we don't really have a product, and it stops him in his tracks.

He can't believe it Well, can you blame him?—Megabux Chemicals, world leaders, marketing something they don't have—but then he sees his 'window of opportunity' as Clare called it. We want a product, he has a product; we want to buy, he wants to sell. He will go away and 'do his arithmetic,' he says, and ring us tomorrow. Meanwhile no-one's to say a word—which suits us fine.

At the end of the meeting, Clare thinks she's solved the problems of the whole world—but I'm not so sure. Must be my background, makes me more suspicious then her. Anyway, we've missed lunch so I volunteer to go round the corner to get us some sarnies—and what do I see on the way but Herr Shoe-thing, in a pub, still wearing his silly Alpine jacket, and he's drinking with a load of mates—and they're laughing a lot. Austrian?—more like New Cross Gate if you ask me.

You could say Clare was not best pleased when I told her. Sir Richard Stuffed-shirt had somehow got wind of what was going on, and had just asked for a 'positive report' by five o'clock that evening. She started talking about hemlock and Socrates. Funny, I thought he was a football player, and she doesn't like football.

Anyway, it didn't come to that, because Herr New Cross Gate wasn't the only one who'd read the Marzipal announcement and wondered what it was all about. I took the call. It was one of our American research labs, 'curious to know where we'd gotten the cute name from'—much better than EZB3 which is what they'd called it. What? Yes, they'd sent details to head office some time back and thought it had been lost among the other computer junk that arrives here...

Clare went all dramatic—"If this were played upon a stage now, I could condemn it as an improbable fiction," says she. More to the point, said I, what's Sir Shining Knight going to do with us, now he doesn't need us to keep his secret any more?

And sure enough, next day we were out, and out for Good. That's Good with a capital 'G'—no more London, no more commuting. Sir Richard White Knight covered his embarrassment with a 'substantial financial gratuity' to us which more than sugared the pill, and Clare and me, we started our own little business— teaching people how to use computers. Cheeky, or what?

We still keep in touch with Bruce—in fact he's designing another training course for us now.

And though I'm not one to pry, I'd rather he didn't have a bath while he's doing it this time!

* * *

Author's note:—

I have to come clean on this one. In a previous existence, I was 'Bruce' the consultant, and I did indeed invent Marzipal as part of a 'scenario' training course at a major company in the chemical industry along with their 'Clare', and we did lose an e-mail in the corporate system and wonder where it might have ended up.

But there, all similarity with this story ends—fortunately!

Slim Jim

That photo? It's of me, before I met Millie. You'd bet how much? Don't, you'd lose it. Listen—if you've got a moment I'll tell you the story. It was Millie that did it to me—her with legs like Twiglets and a figure like a tube of Smarties, as we used to say. And one day there she was.

I hardly knew her name—she was just one of the girls who seemed to hang around in the village at the time—but she came up to me there in the street, bold as you like, and asked if I was coming for a work-out. You what? I said. To the aerobics along with me mates, she said, looks like you could do with it. Someone had put her up to it, that's for sure—I never did find out who. You must be joking, I said. I wasn't going to go showing my body off in front of that lot. You could have hidden the whole giggling bunch of them behind a few bamboo poles, and I told her so.

Very funny I don't think, she says—what you need, Jim Jones, is some self-denial.

Now I know I'm not the smartest pig in the pen, but this self-denial bit wasn't anything they'd taught us at school—or if it was, I hadn't been listening at the time. What's that? I said. It's thinking about what you'd like to do and then not doing it, she said. Doesn't sound like much fun, I said. It's not supposed to be, she said, but it makes you feel good. Unlikely, I thought. But there's no arguing with some people—they'll always manage to get the last word in. So off she flounced with her gang of matchstick friends, and I thought that was the end of it.

Funny, I didn't think of myself as fat then—a bit horizontally challenged perhaps. That's what they call it these days, isn't it? And I felt I ought to get sympathy for that, not stick, if you'll pardon the pun. Also, this self-denial didn't seem to be my scene somehow. But

as it happened, I did get the chance to try it out that very afternoon—
self-denial I mean.

It was like this. I used to drink down the *Fox and Pelican* at
lunchtimes, and I'm just on my way there when I see old widow Hunt
coming up the road towards me. Now she's been asking me to do this
job for her for, oh for months now—and fair enough, a bloke's got to
make a living, but mending her fence isn't my idea of an easy earner,
particularly when she owns the biggest Alsatian dog around and lets
him run loose in the garden. She's also a stickler for having a job
done properly—it might be adequate, but it's not good enough for
me—that's her favourite expression, and I'd heard it more times than
I cared to remember.

Anyway there I am, wondering which way to turn to miss her,
when round the corner comes Scraper—that's 'Skyscraper' Jeffs, all
six foot six of him and skinny as an eel. Bingo, says I to myself—I
need the money as much as he does, but let's try a bit of self-denial.
How does it go?: I think I'd like to earn money—in fact I know I'd
like to earn money—but today I shall resist the temptation and let
Scraper earn the money. Millie was right—just thinking about it
made me feel good.

So I let him catch up with me, and all the time there's Mrs Hunt
bearing down on us. Scraper, says I, it's your lucky day—and I
explain to him the best bits of the job she wants doing. What's in it
for you, says he, suspicious as ever. Got too much on already, says I.
Truthful, I thought, if you took Millie's view of me. He's still not
sure though, even when Mrs H arrives, but I make a quick sales pitch
on his behalf, and he gets given the job then and there. What a
prince, I think to myself feeling a bit of pride in what I'd done. But
then it dawns on me that the job he's got isn't the one I wanted to
lose.

You'll manage it easily enough being so tall Mr Jeffs, she tells
him, and it needs a slim man to get into the space there. She's given
him an indoor job, fixing pesky cupboard shelves in an attic, the
lucky bleeder. Then she turns to me. Don't feel neglected Mr Jones,
there's still the garden fence to be mended.

The fence again! It's November, it's cold, it's wet, and it starts to
get dark before a man's had a chance to put down a couple of decent
lunchtime pints and finish his game of darts. Why me? Why can't I
get the warm, dry, cushy jobs? There ought to be a law against it, I
thought—it's discrimination. I mutter a 'thank you' between my
teeth and tell her I'll start some time round about the middle of next
week. Got a lot on at the moment, I say. She throws me a glance that
would have frozen the equator, and moves on up the road without

saying another word. Scraper offers to buy the first round at the *Fox*. So he ought. Some consolation, says I.

But on the way there, who do we meet but Millie and her friends coming back from their class. She gives me another holier-than-thou look, just like Mrs H did. Not going in for more beer are you? she says. What if I am, says I. One of these days you'll not get out of the door again, she says—you'll get stuck like Pooh Bear. It was my turn to say, very funny I don't think. But she went on: they had to starve him for days to get him out—now if only he'd been doing his aerobics...

She's nothing if not persistent, I had to give her that. OK, I get the message, says I. And I did too, but it wasn't so much her nagging, it was more losing that indoor job to Scraper Jeffs. So next week, I find myself down the village hall in my old shorts and singlet, doing musical step-ups surrounded by bean-poles dressed in flashy leotards. I'm the only bloke there—and feeling a right Walter, I can tell you. But with Millie behind me, and the Dragon in front screaming orders like some demented drill sergeant, there wasn't much chance of escaping once I was in.

How did it go, Scraper asked me next day. Bloody shattering mate, I said. So you won't be going again then, he said. And he had a grin so wide I swear you could see which of his teeth were real and which weren't. Not if you paid me, I said—and thought I meant it. We said 'Cheers,' and I remember the beer tasted exceptionally good that day.

So how come I found myself at it again the following week? And the week after that. Millie had this theory that there was a skinny person inside me fighting to get out. Didn't see him on my last X-ray, says I. That's not what I meant and you know it, says she. She tells me about Nigel Lawson—and if he can do it so can you, she says. That didn't mean a lot to me at the time, but she explained. Apparently he slimmed so successfully that he didn't need a front-door key any more—he just slid in through the key-hole!

Well anyway, that's what I told Scraper when we met in the *Fox* next day. Couldn't stop him laughing, not till I mentioned it was his round and mine was a soda and bitters thank you. Soda & bitter? says he. Is that like a bitter shandy? No, I said, it's some drops of red stuff in a glass of soda water. Looks like dentist's mouthwash and doesn't taste much better. Why drink it then? he says. Because I'm blowed if I'm going to flog my guts out doing physical jerks one day and then undo it all drinking beer the next, says I. Well at that he gives me another one of his big cheesy grins. Got you then has she?

he says. No she has not—it's my choice, says I. And at the time I still thought it was.

Mrs Hunt noticed though. A few weeks later she was watching me struggle into her garden with a six-foot square fencing panel. My, Mr Jones, you're looking fitter these days, she said. I grunted something tactful in reply. It's that young lady of yours, she said, getting you in trim at last. Lady of mine? I'm young, free and single, I said, and intend to remain so. I see, says she, but for how long I wonder? And off she goes into the house to make a pot of tea, leaving me wondering too.

Well we've been married a few years now, Millie and me. She's not such a skinny waif these days of course—a couple of kids have seen to that—but she can still show the younger girls a thing or two in the training gym we run. Yes, *we* run. You're talking to Mr Fitness himself now—well, you can see that can't you. So if I book you in on this course you're asking about, you'd better watch it. I'll guarantee you'll come out slimmer, but I can't promise you'll come out single.

First published in 'Writers News', March 1997

Sylvie

Smile the way that Sylvie smiled,
She saw your face and went her ways,
Rejoicing in the afterglow of love,
And turning from your gaze.

Cry the way that Sylvie cried,
Although the rain had washed her face,
She couldn't stay to thank the tear-stained clouds,
But found another place.

Run the way that Sylvie ran,
Her golden tresses flying wild,
The woodland glades abound with shadow forms
And one more mystic child.

Live the way that Sylvie lives,
In bright Elysian fields of green,
Among the host of players not in play
All waiting for their scene.

See the way that Sylvie sees,
With age-wise eyes she understands
How mortal souls live on to strive anew,
And watch from hidden lands.

Presume Nothing

So tell me this, how come if the guy was wearing one of those—what d'you call 'ems?

Tracker patches.

Yeah, one of those tracker patches—how come you can't find him now?

I wish I knew.

I wish you knew too! The whole country wishes you knew. So why don't you know?

They're not infallible.

Obviously they're not infallible. If they were infallible we wouldn't be standing here having this conversation. But somebody thought they were infallible enough to let this guy out among the ordinary decent clean-living people of this country—and now you tell me you don't know where he's got to. Well, do you? No, I see you shaking your head. You've no idea. So what do we do now?

We have surveillance patrols covering all the likely routes out.

Oh, that's great! That's just dandy!—we have one set of hob-nailed carbine-touting misfits searching for another.

They'll have more than carbines I can assure you.

Allow me a little poetic licence, Captain. And I think you're missing my point.

Which is?

I'm not sure I'd trust your patrolmen with my life any more than the guy they're supposed to be looking for.

Silman is not said to be dangerous.

Wonderful—so we're hunting with carbines and 'more than carbines' for a guy who's 'not said to be dangerous.' Anything else?

He's a serious threat to the community—I don't need to tell you that.

Not dangerous, but a threat to the community. Did they teach you logic at college, Captain?

With respect, Senator, there is a difference.

You bet there's a difference. The difference is that the guy we're after doesn't go around armed to the teeth and killing people—that's what your men are trained to do.

We have women in the patrol too.

Worse. Give a woman a man's job and she'll be out to prove herself. Captain, what I'm saying is, we need to take a more subtle approach to all this. Use our heads, not our hardware.

There's a standard procedure for a bust-out, and we followed it.

This was not a bust-out. The guy was legitimately on the street.

He's a category 'B' criminal, and he's gone missing. Technically that's a bust-out.

Says who?

Says the State law, Senator—you should know that.

So I should. And what *you* should know is that I could take you to this guy right now.

Say that again!

I mean it. While you and your armed guards-persons are all busy following Guideline A, Subsection B, Paragraph C down to the last comma, anyone with half a brain could tell you that you're wasting your time.

If you have information which you've been withholding from us, Senator...

The only information I have is that the sky is blue, the trees are green, and the sun rises in the east. There—now I've made a clean breast of it!

Sir, a fugitive is on the run, and getting further away every second we stand here. Now if you will excuse me...

I will not excuse you, Captain, from using your head. Sit down.

With respect, sir...

Sit down! Or go back out there and look a darned fool. Please. Yes, the comfortable chair—this could take a while. Thank you. Now, have you any idea who this guy is—the one you're searching for?

Silman? We've got his form.

His form. And what's on his form?

Plenty. He got six years.

For?

You name it—embezzlement, fraud, malpractice...

And sneaking on a Senator.

They got Donaldson at the same time, sure.

Not for long though. He was acquitted on a technicality if I remember. Had friends in the right places.

If you say so. Wasn't my case.

But Silman got the full sentence.

Sure, till they 'patched' him out on the trial release last year.

It's still regarded as a full sentence.

Yeah, guess so.

You don't sound convinced.

Wouldn't be my decision.

What would you do? The prisons are bursting at the seams.

Build more prisons—seems logical. We bust a gut to haul the bums in, and now they let them out again.

Too expensive to build—patches are cheaper.

Till they go missing.

Not they, Captain—only one's gone missing.

So far. Only a matter of time before they all find out how to do it, if you ask me.

I doubt that—Silman was special.

What way, special? Able to reject a skin graft you mean?

No, that's not how it was done.

There you go again! What the hell do you know about all this?

Nothing the world can't see. I have a brain, Silman has a brain— I assume you have one too?

I'm beginning to wonder.

You have a brain, Captain, but you've been trained not to use it.

How's that? Not trained to use my brain?

Trained not to use it, I said. That's different.

I don't see how. What are you trying to tell me?

That you're searching in the wrong place, that's all.

Are you serious?

Just look at the facts. Silman was inside because he'd embarrassed certain people in high places.

If you say so.

I know so, and so would you if you lifted your nose above your form book. Also, how many prisoners were released on the 'patch' trial? Just half a dozen—a very small sample, but Silman was among them.

So? They had to choose somebody.

Ah, but who were 'they'?

Gee, I don't know. State governors—commissioners—you tell me.

Donaldson for one.

You don't say.

I do say. So what does your form-book tell you now?

Nothing, I guess. We've got no form on Donaldson anyhow.

He made sure of that. But if we indulge in a little lateral thinking, Captain...

A little what?

Call it putting a side bet on Donaldson. I'd risk a few dollars in that direction.

He's clean—we can't touch him.

Don't need to. Just keep your eyes on him. He'll take you there—all the way.

Senator, it's really not that easy...

Who said it was easy? You get paid for having an easy life? I pay my taxes for that?

So you want me to call off the armed patrols?

No—let them carry on frightening old ladies at check points. Don't want anyone to know we've changed our plan. Just try to make sure they don't shoot anyone, that's all—and put your soft-shoe men onto Donaldson.

I'll need authority.

My authority's all you need. This has to be clandestine—you understand that.

I understand nothing, Senator.

But you'll go along with it.

Listen, let me get this straight. A convicted criminal somehow escapes from surveillance and disappears—that's what's happened— and you're asking me, on your own authority and no-one else's, to set up a tap on some other guy, some clean guy, who you think might possibly, just possibly, have an interest in him. Not only that, but this other guy is also a Senator.

And not in my party, so you're beginning to suspect my motives here.

You said it, not me.

That's fair enough, Captain—I understand—so I suggest you go away now and carry on scouring the district for Silman with your armed heavies. And I hope you have better luck than you've had so far. By the way, what's happened to the others with patches?

We've taken them in again until we know what went wrong with Silman.

So it's the end of the experiment. Very convenient.

Convenient? Who for?

That's for you to find out—you don't trust the information I give you.

Senator, I...

No need to apologize, Captain—you're doing your duty as you see it.

I am, sir.

Then we'll shake hands on it and each get along with our business. There. And now if you'd be so kind as to shut the door on your way out...

* * *

Let's hope that's made him think just enough, but not too much. He'll find plenty on Donaldson to keep himself busy for a while. I should know—I put it there. And when no-one finds Silman, it'll kill the tracker patch idea dead in its tracks too—for a good few years at least. Can't force these things through against public opinion in a democracy.

Loretta, bring me the file on public building programmes will you—my tenders for the new Federal Reform Centres. Yeah, I know it was all shelved, but I'd like to see them again anyway—you never know your luck. Oh, and if the crematorium rings about my cousin's ashes, I'd like them sent here—for safe keeping. We were very close you know, and kept in touch till the end.

Twelfth Night – Act VI

Malvolio: I'll be revenged on the whole pack of you.
Olivia: He hath been most notoriously abused.
Duke: Pursue him, and entreat him to a peace.

Act VI Scene 1—A Room in Olivia's House

He slammed the door shut, threw himself on his bed, and wept. Yes, he, the proud steward of the house, the master and mentor of several dozen cooks, chambermaids, grooms, gardeners, servants and messengers, and the most trusted envoy of the Lady Olivia, wept like a child.

How had he let himself be led into such a ridiculous situation? "Gulled into a nayword," Maria had said. The scheming little bitch. It had been her idea to prepare that letter and leave it where he would be sure to find it. She had written it, copying Lady Olivia's handwriting—it was obvious now—enticing him to dress up in absurd, old-fashioned clothes—yellow stockings and cross-garters, for heavens sake—in the mistaken impression that his Lady had requested it. He had even been fooled by it into thinking that his Lady loved him—him, a commoner! And now he was the laughing stock of all Illyria; worse, of the house and all his subordinates.

He struck at the wood of the bed with his fists, and was glad it hurt. He hated them all, the plotters and the participators, the schemers and the spectators—but most of all, he hated himself. Pride, he realised, was the deadly sin he most possessed, and he had fallen into a crazy snare set by those who recognised his faults. Now his mind surged with fragmented thoughts of furious revenge.

With an oath he bounded off the bed and crossed the room to the pitcher of water standing in its bowl. He would not resign, he told himself as he washed his face to remove any traces of childish grief.

He, Malvolio, would stand and confront the world to prove he was stronger in spirit than the sniggering fools surrounding him. But first he needed to calm down. He dried himself on a cloth, threw it to one side and returned to sit on his bed. Then gently, he pulled from underneath a lavishly decorated green velvet sack, placed this on his knees, and folded it back lovingly to reveal his most treasured possession.

* * *

Maria had not immediately obeyed the order to follow him. After all, she reasoned, it came from the Duke's mouth and he was not her master. But she also realised that this was merely finding an excuse for delaying the inevitable meeting. Lady Olivia had signalled approval with her eyes, and was unlikely to feel the need to add verbally to the Duke's request.

The plain truth was that Maria felt silly. In the heat of the moment, plotting the device with those half-drunken old men and that idiot of a Fool, she had been confident enough. But it had worked almost too successfully, and the victim had been too completely demolished by it. She found herself, unexpectedly, feeling sorry for him as she approached his suite down the long side-corridor. She rehearsed words to herself: 'Our Mistress wishes to speak with us', or 'Our Mistress entreats you to peace'. She expected a firm rebuttal, and thought morosely that it would need all her tact and guile to get him even to open the door. What she had not expected however was to hear the sound of soft music coming from the end of the corridor— lilting and lyrical, and unmistakably from the hands of a practised musician—the alluring tones of a lute playing a stately galliard.

She paused to listen, then drew closer to the door—his door. She assumed he had a visitor. That would be awkward, given the delicate nature of her mission. Then, reasoning that the presence of another person might at least prevent her from being abused on the doorstep, she took a deep breath and knocked. The music stopped at once, but in the silence that followed there was no answer. Hesitantly, she knocked again.

"Who is it?" The voice had regained all its old authority, and Maria found her legs shaking involuntarily.

"Maria"—then quickly, "I have a message from the Mistress."

She heard footsteps within the room, but not heading immediately in her direction; a pause, and then they approached and the latch was lifted. The door opened a bare inch, and through the gap their eyes met—the gulled and the gull-catcher, the master and the maid. For a full score of heartbeats, not a word was spoken. His unblinking, level stare beat fiercely upon the nervous, downcast face of Maria, her eyes darting, first this way, then that.

"Well?"

"From the Mistress," she repeated anxiously.

"So you said." He waited. He was not going to make this an easy interview.

"She would like to see you—us..." Her voice trailed away, undecided as to what else to say.

"My Mistress sent you to tell me this?"

Maria evaded answering the question by changing the subject: "But I am sure she was not aware that you had a visitor," she said.

"A visitor?" He seemed genuinely puzzled. "I have no visitor."

"But the beautiful music," said Maria, "I thought..."

A look of irritation flashed across his face—she had heard!—then the beginnings of a faint smile—she had thought it beautiful. "I have no visitor," he repeated in softer tones, unconsciously opening the door a little wider as he spoke.

"Then—it was you?"

"Indeed—I. You were not aware I had talents other than those used in the course of my domestic duties."

"I—I thought it was a musician playing," she said earnestly. Then quickly, not wanting to imply any criticism, "I mean a real musician."

At this, Malvolio laughed sharply. "Am I not real enough for you?"

Maria blushed, but decided not to compound her embarrassment by trying to talk her way out of it. The door was now fully open, and she could see the lute lying on the bed. He followed her gaze with his.

"It belonged to my father," he said. "I learnt from him. Now he was a real musician."

Maria looked up, and in his eyes there was a softness and a contentment she had never seen there before. "May I?," she asked, indicating the instrument.

"My Mistress may become impatient waiting for us," he said with an unaccustomed glint in his eye.

"I just wanted to look at it," she replied innocently. Then suddenly realizing where they were, her scullery sense of humour reasserted itself, and she roared with laughter, and Malvolio, the once proud, stiff steward of the house, laughed heartily with her and conducted her into his room. Then, picking up the lute with care, he handed it to her, and she held it as if it was a new-born baby, turning it gently in her hands to admire the workmanship.

"Do you play?," he asked.

"I? No!," she replied, "At least, not the lute." She handed it back to him. "Will you play me some of the piece I heard when I arrived?"

He sat down, held the instrument with a natural ease, and once more the haunting notes of the galliard filled the room. His fingers moved gracefully across the strings, and his eyes focused on a distant imaginary point as the power of the music took hold of him. He was oblivious of the room, of the house, of the time, and did not notice as Maria reached into her pocket to bring out what seemed like a large shell and put it to her lips. Only when he heard the sound of a sweet descant rising, falling and weaving around his own melody did he realise he was not the only musician in the room. Then his face lit up, and his playing became even more lyrical, as Maria on her ocarina kept company with him.

They ended the piece with a flourish, and for a moment neither spoke. Then, wistfully, he said, "You are as good a musician as you are a forger of letters."

"You'll never forgive me for that."

"I thought not." He paused, then: "I might have to move away."

"No!" Her reply was more urgent than she had intended it to be, but perhaps he had not noticed.

"Do you think that I can maintain the dignity of my position in this household after today's events?"

"Those who did it to you were fools."

He gave her a look and smiled. "Not all—and I am honest enough to admit now that there was some justification in it."

"The dignity of your position obscured the disposition of your dignity."

"Now there's a construction worthy of the Fool," he said.

She put the ocarina back in her pocket. "I mean I think your position is secure if only you would unbend a little," she said.

"With your help, I can try," said he. Then, hesitantly: "They tell me Sir Toby has offered you his hand in marriage."

"Hah! Which meddler told you that? Any wife of his would spend all her life carrying the sot to bed."

"It's a false report then?"

"Spread about by himself more in hope than in expectation, I'll wager. Why do you ask?"

"No pressing reason—pure curiosity. Come, our Lady will be sending for us if we don't go shortly," and he held out his arm for her.

She slipped her arm in his, and they walked together through the corridors of the house back towards Olivia's chamber. "She is absorbed in the plans for her wedding," said Malvolio. "No doubt she will be glad to see we have managed a reconciliation of our own."

"Surprised though," Maria said with a giggle, already relishing the gasps their entry would create. "Who'd have thought it?"

"Who indeed."

The wedding was planned for three weeks time. Later, at Lady Olivia's wedding, the happy couple were asked by her to provide the music to entertain her guests. All who heard it commented on the remarkable partnership shown by the two musicians, and the Duke, never one to discard a good line, was heard to exclaim once again:

"If music be the food of love, play on."

I Survived in Grayshott

I'm sure we all know at least one place where the Highway Code seems to be a foreign document. Grayshott is a lovely place, but…

I've travelled over all this sceptred isle
From John o' Groats to Lands End, and the way's not
Notable for trouble or delay
Unless, that is, you're coming back through Grayshott.

When driving homeward, mile on solid mile
From Lord knows where, I find the thing I pray's not,
"Let there be no freezing rain today",
But, "Let there be no silly bods in Grayshott".

    Grayshott grew from gorse and heather,
    Snug by Hindhead and built for humanity;
    Yet it somehow altogether
    Lacks a sense of Highway Code sanity.

So, stuck in jams or crawling single file
Through contraflows near Leeds, I know my day's not
Reached its nadir till I've joined the fray
To drive the last frustrating mile through Grayshott.

Then, safely home, in celebration I'll
Consume a calming toast; and though today's not
Likely to be famed in any other way,
To me it's something—I survived in Grayshott!

About the Author

John Owen Smith, commonly known as 'Jo', was born in 1942 and educated as a scientist. He had very little serious interest in writing fiction until he started to write pantomime scripts for his local amateur dramatic company in Headley, Hampshire, in the late 1980s. Out of this came a commission to write a historical community play, and from that emerged a whole new career as a local historian, publisher and occasional writer and dramatist.

The pieces included in this book were written over a period of twelve years or so, and come from a variety of inspirations. The majority are short stories written for recreation and entered in competitions run by *Writers News* magazine. One (*Jobsworth*) is adapted from the first in a series of six radio plays written by the author about the mythical life of a caretaker. *Marzipal* is an outrageous fiction from a mundane real-life event. And others entries are verses written at different times and on various themes.

About the Publisher

John Owen Smith, commonly known as 'Jo', was born in 1942 and educated as a … *but you already know that!*

I started self-publishing in 1993 of necessity, when I needed to produce a book quickly in time to meet a tight deadline (to coincide with the community play mentioned above). It was a success and proved to me that, at least as far as local history is concerned, self-publishing was the route to follow – and I've been doing it ever since.

At first, print runs of several thousand copies were needed to be economic, which was not ideal, but the situation improved greatly when 'print on demand' became generally available around 2000; and has improved even more now that on-line facilities are offered by the likes of CreateSpace.com where it literally cost nothing to set up a book for publication.

For further information about me, my work and my publications,
including plays and pantomimes for performance,
have a look at my website www.johnowensmith.co.uk
or contact me at wordsmith@johnowensmith.co.uk

Heatherley *by Flora Thompson*
Her lost sequel to **Lark Rise to Candleford** in which she tells of her time in Hampshire at the beginning of the 19th century after leaving 'Candleford Green.'
ISBN 978-1-873855-29-4

The Peverel Papers *by Flora Thompson*
Nature Notes 1921–27 from the author of **Lark Rise** written while she lived in Liphook. Published here in full and in a single edition for the first time.
ISBN 978-1-873855-57-7

Flora Thompson, the Story of the 'Lark Rise' Writer – *a biography by Gillian Lindsay*
Anyone who has enjoyed Flora Thompson's books will appreciate the opportunity to learn more about this exceptional woman.
ISBN 978-1-873855-53-9

On the Trail of Flora Thompson *by John Owen Smith*. The author of **Lark Rise** lived for nearly 30 years 'beyond Candleford Green' in Hampshire. This book tells of the people and places she met while living locally in Grayshott and Liphook.
ISBN 978-1-873855-24-9

Grayshott *by J.H. Smith*
The history of Grayshott from its earliest beginnings as a minor hamlet of Headley to its status as a fully independent parish flourishing on the borders of Hampshire and Surrey in the 20th century.
ISBN 978-1-873855-38-6

The Hilltop Writers *by W.R. Trotter*
In which we meet Tennyson, Conan Doyle, Bernard Shaw and sixty-three other writers who populated the hilltops around Haslemere and Hindhead at the end of the 1890s.
ISBN 978-1-873855-31-7

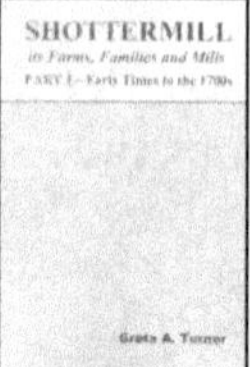

Shottermill, its farms, Families and Mills *by Greta Turner* Two volumes covering the history of this community in the Wey valley from its earliest days up to the start of the 20th century.
ISBN 978-1-873855-39-3
ISBN 978-1-873855-40-9

Headley's Past in Pictures *by John Owen Smith* Three illustrated tours of Headley parish in old photographs: in the village centre and Arford; to Headley Down and beyond; and along the River Wey and its tributaries.
ISBN 978-1-873855-27-0

One Monday in November *by John Owen Smith* The Selborne & Headley 'Swing' riots of 1830, their dramatic events and their after-effects are recounted from the known facts and often contradictory reports and legends which have grown up since.
ISBN 978-1-873855-33-1

All Tanked Up *by John Owen Smith* Tells of the 'invasion' of Headley by Canadian tank regiments during WW2, told from the point of view of both Villagers and Canadians. Including details of the regiments involved.
ISBN 978-1-873855-54-6

A Parcel of Gold for Edith *by Joyce Stevens* The story of Ellen Suter, an Australian Pioneer Woman, who fled the poverty of England and set off alone, aged only 19, to live in the new colony of Victoria on the other side of the world.
ISBN 978-1-873855-36-2

A Headley Compendium *by John Owen Smith* A republication of Canon Tudor Jones' well-researched book *Headley 1066–1966* and material previously published in the *Headley Miscellany* series of booklets.
ISBN 978-1-873855-62-1

Pantomimes & Plays by John Owen Smith

Full length pantomimes (2 acts) with one interval:

- **Aladdin** The pantomime with the flying palace – 15 speaking parts + chorus
- **Ali Baba** Scheherazade introduces her very last Arabian Night's tale – 18 speaking parts + chorus
- **Cinderella** Baron Hardup's household as tradition tells it – with immortal lines – 14 speaking parts + chorus
- **Dick Whittington** and his cat – the tale as recorded by Fred Chaucer – 16 speaking parts + chorus
- **Humpty Dumpty** The Muffet Mob's on the loose – can old egghead save the day? – 16 speaking parts + 7 children speaking + chorus
- **Jack and the Beanstalk** Witch Whey's wicked wheeze won't work – will it? – 17 speaking parts + chorus
- **Nutcracker** The script Tchaikovsky might have set to music, if he'd known – 15 speaking parts + chorus
- **Puss in Boots** That talking cat gets everywhere – and gets his just desserts! – 15 speaking parts + chorus
- **Little Red Riding Hood** There could be a fete worse than death – ask the Wolf! – 16 speaking parts + chorus
- **Robin Hood** A cricket match in Sherwood Forest? There's Nun Better to play – 15 speaking parts + chorus
- **Sleeping Beauty** The show with an interval of a hundred years! – 11 speaking parts + chorus
- **Snow White and the 7 Dwarfs** The mirror's off the wall in more ways than one! – 18 speaking parts + chorus

Mini Pantomimes (in verse): **approx 15-20 mins run time**

- **Cinderelder** Prince Charming gets a bit fed up with Cinderella after 20 years! – 9 speaking parts
- **Bleeding Moody** Can you imagine the Sleeping Beauty as a teenager of today? – 6 speaking parts

Full length plays (2 acts) with one interval:

- **Flora's Heatherley** An historical play based on Flora Thompson's time in Grayshott 1898–1901 – 20 speaking parts
- **Flora's Peverel** An historical play based on Flora Thompson's time in Liphook 1916–1928 – 25 speaking parts
- **The Broomsquire** Adapted from the novel by Sabine Baring-Gould – 20 speaking parts (can be performed by 10 people)
- **MacHamlet** A Shakespearean comedy – 21 speaking parts
- **Bard Again!** MacHamlet takes to foreign parts – 21 speaking parts
- **MacHamlet Goes West!** and meets a Tempest – 23 speaking parts